"GET LOST, FRIEND."

The man's voice sounded like his last meal had been ground glass.

"Mr. Adams," Banbury said, "p-please. These gentlemen mean me no harm."

Ground Glass belied the remark by choosing that moment to backhand Banbury across the mouth. The small man's bottom lip split, and the blood ran down his chin.

Clint watched all three men. "Okay, that's it. Fun time is over. Let him go."

"What's got into you, mister?" Ground Glass asked. "This ain't none of your affair."

"I'm making it mine," Clint said. "Now let him go."

"Mister," Ground Glass said, "just in case you can't count there's three of us. You gonna gun us? All three?"

"One, two, three," Clint said with a shrug. "It's all the same to me."

THE GUNSMITH

207

KANSAS CITY KILLING

J. R. ROBERTS

J

JOVE BOOKS, NEW YORK

KANSAS CITY KILLING

A Jove Book / published by arrangement with the author

PRINTING HISTORY
Jove edition / April 1999

For information address: The Berkley Publishing Group, a member of Penguin Putnam Inc., 375 Hudson Street, New York, New York 10014.

The Penguin Putnam Inc. World Wide Web site address is http://www.penguinputnam.com

ISBN: 0-515-12486-9

A JOVE BOOK®
Jove Books are published by The Berkley Publishing Group, a member of Penguin Putnam Inc., 375 Hudson Street, New York, New York 10014.
JOVE and the "J" design are trademarks belonging to Jove Publications, Inc.

PRINTED IN THE UNITED STATES OF AMERICA

10 9 8 7 6 5 4 3 2 1

ONE

When Clint Adams rode into Kansas City he knew nothing about the Fancy Man. He didn't know that there was such a store or that it was causing a stir not only in Kansas City but throughout the region. And he didn't know that he'd soon be playing a part in that stir.

Past run-ins with men like Jesse and Frank James as well as friends like Bat Masterson, had brought Clint to Kansas City from time to time. In fact, some recent trouble involving his friend Luke Short had brought Clint there recently, but not for any length of time, so he hadn't had a chance to look around. Now, on his way back from another part of Missouri, he decided to stop in for a more leisurely visit.

Kansas City had often been the site of troubles, and its citizens had banded together before, but never with the fervor with which they were now banding together against the Fancy Man.

Clint did the things he usually did when visiting a town: made sure Duke was properly cared for, got himself a room at a hotel—in this case, the Kansas House—and then went in search of a cold beer. In this case, he chose a saloon on Broadway called the Shady Lady.

The saloon had not been in Kansas City the last time he

was there, so he entered curiously. He immediately saw the painting over the bar, a silhouette of a well-endowed woman—full of bust and behind—obviously naked. The fellow manning the bar beneath it looked inordinately proud to be there; he greeted Clint expansively, causing Clint to wonder if he treated all his customers this way, or just those who were obviously new.

"What can I get you, friend?" he inquired.

"A cold beer would be nice," Clint said.

"Comin' up."

Clint took the opportunity to look around. Covered gaming tables hinted at the business the place would be doing later in the day. Right now there were only a few men in the place, busy with their beers or their whiskeys.

He turned as the bartender put his beer on the bar.

"How do you get away with that?" Clint asked.

"You mean her?" The bartender jerked his thumb behind him. "The Shady Lady?"

"That's what I mean." Clint figured the man must have gotten asked that a lot. He'd known immediately what Clint was getting at.

"I got lucky," the bartender said. Obviously, he was the owner of the place.

"How so?"

"Well, I used to have to fight for that painting every day," he said. "Women in town hated it. You know what I said?"

"What?"

"I tol' 'em, you don't like it, don't come in here. Women don't belong in my place, anyway—unless they're workin' here, know what I mean?"

"I know."

"Well, they complained that they could see it through the window when they went by. They also complained that it gave their husbands ideas, you know?"

Clint nodded. He hated talking to people who punctuated their remarks with "you know?" all the time, but he'd also learned that there was no way to break them of the habit.

"So what happened?"

"My luck," the man said, "was when the women in this town found somethin' else to complain about."

"And what was that?"

The man smiled, leaned an elbow on the bar, and said, "The Fancy Man."

Clint waited, but there was apparently no explanation coming.

"And what's that? A person or a place?"

"Both."

"Both?"

The man nodded happily.

"I'm afraid you're confusing me, friend."

"Fella came to town," the bartender said, "and opened up a store. It's on one of the side streets. Probably why you didn't see it when you rode in."

"Probably."

"Well sir, when the women in this town saw what he was sellin' they just about went crazy."

"What kind of store is it?" Clint asked.

The bartender straightened up and stared at Clint.

"You got to see it to believe it, friend."

Clint was curious enough now to want to do that.

"Well, where is it?"

"Two blocks south, take a right, you can't miss it," the man said. "Thirteenth Street."

"And what's it called?"

"I tol' ya," the bartender said. "The Fancy Man."

Clint finished his beer, set the empty mug down, and settled up with the man. "South, two blocks, make a right," he repeated.

"You got it," the bartender said. "Come back and tell me what ya think. If ya do, I'll give ya a beer on the house."

"You got a deal," Clint said, and left to go find the Fancy Man.

TWO

Clint wondered how he was going to find what he was looking for when he didn't know what he was looking for. He found what he thought was the street and turned down it. As soon as he did it became fairly evident what he was looking for.

Ahead of him people were studiously avoiding something, crossing the street to get away from it. In some cases women were hiding their eyes. Clint walked down the block and finally found out what the Fancy Man was.

It was a store, and judging from what was on display in the window, it sold women's underwear—but these undergarments were unlike anything Clint had ever seen in his life. *Ever*—not even in a whorehouse.

The items in the window, when worn by a woman, would not hide much of her natural charms. They would either be pushed up and out or revealed through cutouts. Clint looked around self-consciously, because he found himself imagining a few women he knew wearing some of these items.

"Well," a man said, "at least you're not running away."

Clint looked at the doorway and saw a small, dapper, well-dressed, and impeccably barbered man.

"I don't see anything here that might bite me," Clint replied.

"Very progressive thinking on your part, sir," the man said. "I'd introduce myself, but that would necessitate shaking hands, and that might make you unwanted in this town."

"I'll chance it."

"Excellent!" the man exclaimed, looking happy. He stuck out his hand. "Harrison C. Banbury, haberdasher by trade."

Clint shook his hand. "Clint Adams. I take it, then, that you own this place? You're the Fancy Man?"

"Oh, no," Banbury said. "I simply run the store. The owner is back in Chicago. He is Andrew B. Robinson, of the Wilmette Robinsons. Surely you've heard of him?"

"I have not," Clint said, "no."

"Well, sir, he is the Fancy Man, not I. I just happen to run this particular store."

"There are others?"

"Oh, my, yes," Banbury said. "I have some very good coffee on my stove, sir. Would you care for some?"

"I'm always ready for good coffee," Clint said.

"Good and strong?"

"The only kind."

"Come in, then," Banbury said. "I don't expect we'll be interrupted by a customer any time soon."

Clint followed Banbury into the store, where more garments of the same type were on display.

"If you don't mind my asking," Clint said, "why are you open if you don't expect any customers?"

"Allow me to pour the coffee," Banbury said, "and then we can talk."

Clint waited while Banbury poured two cups and handed one to him. He tasted it, and as advertised, it was excellent.

"To answer your question," Banbury began, "we—that is, Mr. Robinson—opened seven of these stores just last month. One here, one each in Denver, Sacramento, Chicago, New York, and Boston. Is that seven?"

"Six."

"Six?" The man frowned. "I've forgotten one. Ah, yes . . . Philadelphia. We don't expect to do any business at all for the first few months, because it will take people that long to get used to our, er, merchandise."

"And your Mr. Robinson, he has enough money to operate these stores at a loss for that period of time?"

"Oh, my, yes," Banbury said, "or longer. Oh, yes, we are very well financed in this endeavor."

The way the man said "we" made Clint wonder if there were more to his involvement than he was saying.

"Look around," Banbury continued. "If you see something you think a ladyfriend will like, I'll make you a gift of it."

Clint walked to the window in time to see a young woman looking into it. When she saw him she quickly averted her eyes and scurried off. He wondered just how many months it would take for people to decide it was safe to look and buy without being damned to hell.

"Anything?" Banbury asked.

Clint turned and smiled.

"Not right now."

"Well," Banbury said, "the offer stands. Come back any time."

"Why?" Clint asked. "Why me?"

"Because," Banbury said, "you're the first person in this town who didn't treat me like I had the plague."

"A good enough reason, I guess," Clint said. He finished the coffee and held the cup out to his host. "Thanks for the coffee."

"My door is always open," Banbury said.

"What about your wife?" Clint asked. "Does she wear any of . . . this?"

"I'm not married," Banbury said. "As to having a woman who could wear some of this, I wish I had. I suspect you have, in the past."

"Maybe." Clint smiled.

"Ah," Banbury said. "I see from your face you *have* had such a woman."

"I have to go."

"Will you be in town long?"

"A few days, maybe."

"Ah, good," Banbury said. "We'll be seeing one another again, then."

Clint simply nodded, smiled, and walked out.

THREE

There was a café across the street from the Fancy Man. Clint went over and easily got a table by the window. The waiter explained to him that since "that store" opened across the street no one ever sat at the window tables anymore.

"Why not?" Clint wanted to know.

"What do you mean, why not?" the middle-aged man asked. "That window across the street, it's . . . it's . . . obscene."

"Do you really think so?"

"Don't you?" the man asked, shocked.

"No, I don't," Clint said. "In fact, I know some women who would look mighty good in some of those items."

"Well, of course," the man said, "*those* kinds of women!"

"What kind is that?"

"Well, you know," the man said. "Whores."

"Have you ever been to a whorehouse?"

"I'm a married man!" The waiter looked around, as if someone had been trying to trap him with that question.

"So you've *never* been to a whorehouse?"

"Well . . . of course . . . when I was younger . . . and *single*," he hastily pointed out.

"And what about your wife?"

"What about her?"

"Is she an attractive woman?"

"I like to think so."

"Wouldn't she look nice in one of those items? In the privacy of your own bedroom, of course."

"Well, I suppose so . . . but that window is not private. It's there for everyone to see."

Clint frowned. He couldn't argue with that.

"I'll have a pot of coffee and a piece of peach pie," he said instead.

"Cup of coffee—" the man started to repeat.

"A *pot* of coffee."

"A pot of coffee," the man said, writing it down, "and a piece of peach pie. Right away, sir."

Clint looked out the window while he waited, watching men and women alike avert their eyes and cross to the other side of the street to get away from the window. But he noticed something. Even though the store had opened last month and people knew it was there, they still waited until they were right in front of the window to react. In other words, they were taking their look first, then averting their eyes.

A bunch of hypocrites, Clint thought. Banbury was probably right. Inside of three months these hypocrites would be shopping in the store.

Clint finished his pie and coffee, watching the street the whole time. It was unlike him to sit at a window table, making an easy target of himself, but he made an exception in this instance. He found himself fascinated by this situation. He was sure that half the men in Kansas City had been to whorehouses; maybe five or ten percent of the women had been whores, for all he knew. He knew that half of them couldn't be virgins, so why were they acting so scandalized? The men to impress the women? The women to impress the men? *"Look at me, dear, I'm embarrassed."*

It was all pretty ridiculous. He wondered how the people of New York and Boston were reacting. And Denver. Had his friend Talbot Roper seen the store? What did he think about it? If Clint knew Roper he'd already bought half a dozen items for the women he was seeing.

He was waiting to pay his bill when he saw three men stop in front of the store, look in the window, and then go inside. They were all dressed alike, trail clothes and holsters. Not the type of men you'd see go into a store that was, essentially, for women.

He left the money on the table and hurried across the street, smelling trouble the whole way.

FOUR

Clint stopped just outside the store, looking in through the glass of the door. The three men were handling merchandise, tossing it around, and Harrison C. Banbury didn't seem able to do anything to stop them. Clint thought for a moment that as long as they were only throwing around some women's underwear there was no reason for him to butt in, but at that moment one of the men reached out and grabbed the smaller man by his shirt.

Clint opened the door and stepped inside.

"We're closed, friend," one of the men said.

"Yeah," the second said, "takin' inventory." He threw a corset across the store to the first man.

The third man, the one holding onto Banbury, was the biggest and had the meanest eyes of the bunch.

"Get lost, friend," he growled. His voice sounded like his last meal had been ground glass.

"I'm looking for something for my lady friend," Clint said. "Can any of you gents help me?"

"Yeah," the first man said. "We can help you out the door."

"Mr. Adams," Banbury said, "p-please. These gentlemen mean me no harm."

Ground Glass belied the remark by choosing that moment to backhand Banbury across the mouth. The small man's bottom lip split, and the blood ran down his chin.

"Shut up!" Ground Glass ordered.

Clint watched all three men, and when the first two each had an item of clothing in their hands he said, "Okay, that's it. Fun time is over. Let him go."

"What did you say?" Ground Glass asked.

The first two men started to put the clothing down but Clint snapped, "Don't. Just hold onto those items, boys." He pointed with his left hand when he spoke, his right hanging near his gun.

"What's got into you, mister?" Ground Glass asked. "This ain't none of your affair."

"I guess I'm making it mine," Clint said. "Now let him go."

The man did so, contemptuously pushing Banbury away from him. The smaller man staggered and caught himself on a display case, regaining his feet.

"Mister," Ground Glass said, "just in case you can't count there's three of us."

"I can count."

"We can take you apart and toss you through that there window."

"You might," Clint agreed, "if I let you get that close."

"You gonna gun us?" the man asked. "All three?"

"That's your choice."

"He means it, Les," the first man said to Ground Glass.

"Les?" Clint asked. "Les what?"

"What's it to you?"

"I usually like to know a man's name before I have to kill him," Clint said.

"Damn," the second man said, "he does mean it. He'll draw on the three of us."

The first two men didn't seem to like the fact that the odds didn't distress Clint.

"One, two, three," Clint said with a shrug. "It's all the same to me."

"Hey, Les," the first man said, still holding a frilly number with something fuzzy on it, "he ain't kiddin'. He must be a professional."

"Yeah," Les said, "yeah, I think you're right, Blaine. He has that look."

Clint just stood there and waited, keeping his eyes on the leader, Les.

"Okay, mister," Les finally said, "you called it this time. Step aside and we'll be goin'."

"Lace your fingers behind your heads first."

Les grinned and said, "I ain't gonna do that, friend, but they will. Boys? Oblige the gentleman."

Both men dropped what they were holding and put their hands behind their heads.

"Good enough?" Les asked.

"I guess it'll have to be," Clint said. He moved away from the door. "Okay, get going."

They walked to the door single file. The first man eyed Clint for a moment, then dropped one hand from behind his head just long enough to open the door. The first two men left, but Les stopped just inside the door.

"I'll be seein' you again," he said.

"If you do," Clint replied, "it'll be the last time."

Les grinned again, tightly, then left, closing the door gently behind him.

Harrison C. Banbury's relief was immediate. His legs gave out and he slid to the floor, his back against the display case.

"Are you all right?" Clint asked, crouching down next to him.

"I—yu-yes, I am, I think," he said. "Just allow me to sit here for a moment."

"Do you know who those three were?"

"N-no, I don't."

Clint hesitated a moment before asking the next question.

"Do you know who sent them?"

For a brief moment there was something in Banbury's eyes, and then it faded.

"N-no, I don't—what makes you think they were sent?" he asked.

"Do you think they just stopped in here on their own?"

"I thought they were customers, when they entered."

"They didn't look like customers to me."

"How did you know—"

"I was in the café across the street," Clint said. "I saw them come in and thought I should check."

"Could you help me to my feet?" Banbury asked.

"Sure."

When the man was standing he said, "It's lucky for me you were around. I owe you my thanks."

"That's all right," Clint said. "Maybe I can help you clean up in here."

They looked around; the floor was covered with gauzy, filmy female items.

"That's all right," Banbury said. "I—I'll close and clean up."

"You'll want to see about that lip, too," Clint said.

The bleeding had stopped, but it was still an ugly cut. Banbury touched it and winced, which started it bleeding again.

"Yes," he said, "yes, I will. Thank you again, Mr. Adams. It was . . . quite something to see, the way you forced those men to back down. Were they right?"

"About what?"

"About you," the man said. "Are you a . . . professional?"

"Professional what?"

"I don't—well, I—"

"You should be a little careful from now on, Mr. Banbury."

The man's eyes widened and he asked, "Do you think they'll be back?"

"Maybe," Clint said, "unless whoever sent them calls them off."

"I—well, I don't know what I can—"

"Get yourself a shotgun and keep it behind the counter," Clint advised.

"Oh, I couldn't *shoot* anyone."

"You might not have to. A shotgun is an ugly thing. Just pointing it might do the job," Clint said.

"Yes, well then, perhaps that's what I should do."

"Well, if you're sure you're all right I'll be leaving now."

"Thank you again."

"You better come and lock the door."

As Clint went out the door he waited until the lock clicked, and then Banbury turned his OPEN sign around so it said CLOSED.

For how long? Clint wondered.

FIVE

After they left the Fancy Man, Les Revere dismissed the two men who had been with him and went to report to his employer.

James Wonderly did not live up to his name. When Revere had first met Wonderly he'd been surprised by the man's rather mild-sounding name. Wonderly wore three-piece suits, but looked as if he'd be more comfortable in a boxing ring. In point of fact he had been a wrestler in his younger days, something he continued to brag about now that he was into his fifties. Now, however, his pursuits were less physical and more financial.

Revere didn't know why Wonderly was worried about this Fancy Man store. No one went near it, and as far as Revere knew, nobody had even bought anything since it opened. Still, Wonderly was paying the tab, so when he told Revere to go over to the store and bust it up and the man who worked there, who was he to argue? He'd picked two men that he knew wouldn't mind the work, but they were good with their hands, not their guns; so when that gunman had shown up the smart thing had been to back off.

The thing to do now was explain it to Wonderly.

• • •

James Wonderly twirled the cigar between his lips, wetting it, savoring the taste of it as if it were one of the young women he had brought to him several times a week at his home. His wife slept in a different room, and she knew what it meant when he suggested that she go to it.

Wonderly stared down at Broadway, at the people hustling back and forth. He knew that if he opened the window and spat there was a good chance his spittle would land on someone who was on his payroll. This pleased him enormously—and so did the picture it brought to mind. He was sorely tempted to try it when the door to his office opened and his secretary walked in.

"Mr. Revere is here, Mr. Wonderly," Eileen Wilson announced.

He turned and regarded Miss Wilson with the same enjoyment he'd been expending on his cigar. He'd hired her because she was young, lovely, and full-bodied; but to date he had not yet slept with her. He was saving that pleasure for when the time came to fire her.

"Send him in, darlin'," Wonderly said. He knew she hated it when he called her that, but he was paying her too well for her to complain. This one was going to be a challenge, he thought, as she turned and went back out the door, leaving her heady scent behind. Wonderly seated himself behind the desk he'd had delivered from Philadelphia and set about to lighting his cigar.

Les Revere walked in and Wonderly instantly knew that the job he had assigned to the man had not been done.

"What happened?" he asked wearily.

"Somebody came into the store while we were there," Revere explained.

"Who? A customer? You couldn't get rid of him?"

"This was no customer," Revere said. "He was a hired gun."

Wonderly laughed aloud.

"The Fancy Man has hired a gun?"

"That's what it looks like."

"You sure he didn't just walk in on you by accident?" Wonderly asked.

"He was ready to draw on the three of us if we didn't leave the store."

"And you left?"

"The boys I hired on weren't gunmen."

"And you?"

"I'm no gunny, either," Revere said. "You might have to hire somebody who is."

Wonderly twirled the cigar between his lips as he considered this turn of events.

"Do you know who the man was?"

"No," Revere said, "but the fancy dan who works there called him Adams."

"Adams," Wonderly said, then shook his head and said, "Nah, couldn't be."

"Clint Adams?" Revere asked.

"That's what I was thinking," Wonderly said, "but why would he get involved in this?"

"I never heard that he actually hired his gun out," Revere said, "but maybe that's wrong."

"Maybe."

"Whataya gonna do?"

"Do you know somebody?" Wonderly asked. "Somebody good with a gun?"

"I know a few fellas."

"Get in touch with them. See if they're available."

"For what you can pay," Revere said, "I guarantee they'll be available."

Wonderly waved the hand that was holding the cigar, making designs in the air with the smoke.

"Don't make an offer, yet," he said. "I also want you to find out if that man was, indeed, Clint Adams. Can you do that, Mr. Revere?"

"I can do it."

"More efficiently than you did this little job for me?" Wonderly said pointedly.

Revere bit back a hasty reply that might have cost him money and repeated, "I can do it."

Wonderly again waved the hand holding the cigar, this time in a dismissive gesture. "Then do it."

SIX

Clint went back to the Shady Lady saloon. He figured to cash in on that free beer, and maybe get some more information.

As he approached the bar the bartender saw him and grinned.

"One beer comin' up," the man said, "on the house."

Clint waited while the man drew the beer and set it down in front of him.

"Did you see what I meant?" he asked.

"In more ways than one."

"Whataya mean?"

Clint took a good swallow of the cold beer and then told the man what happened. He finished by wondering aloud who was so worried about the Fancy Man that he'd send three men to do some damage, and maybe more.

"That'd be ol' Jim Wonderly," the bartender said.

"Wonderly?"

"Well, he ain't so old," the barkeep said, "probably about my age—fifty or so—but he sure has accomplished more in his life than I have in mine."

"A rich man, is he?"

"And then some."

"So why would he worry about the Fancy Man?"

"Because Jim Wonderly is a businessman," the bartender said. "He knows a good thing when he sees it."

"So you think *he* thinks the store will be a success," Clint said, "and he doesn't want it in town?"

"That's one way of looking at it."

"And what's another way?"

The man leaned his elbows on the bar and said, "He wants to buy in."

"And they don't need his money."

"Right."

"So he'll make them need . . . what? His protection?"

"Maybe," the man said, straightening up. "Hey, if I had all the answers maybe Wonderly would be here swabbing this bar and I'd be livin' in that big house with a wife and a bunch of mistresses."

"He cheats on his wife?"

"I'll bet," the bartender said. "James Wonderly cheats on everything."

"You seem to know a lot about what goes on," Clint said, and then thought, *Maybe even more than most bartenders.* "What's your name?"

"Chaplin," the bartender said, "Tim Chaplin."

"And you own the Shady Lady?"

"I do."

"What'd you do before you bought this place?"

Chaplin grinned and said, "I was Jim Wonderly's partner."

And that was a whole other story.

"It's not a long story," Chaplin said. "I mean, I got what I deserved."

"How so?"

They were still standing at the bar. Business was starting to pick up around them while Clint nursed the free beer along.

"I knew who I was partnered with," Chaplin explained, "and one day I looked the other way."

"That's all it took?"

"We were partners for five years, and I think he was waiting for that one moment, waiting to catch me off guard."

"What happened?"

"I got out with enough money to buy this place," Chaplin said.

"And you don't hold a grudge?"

"I did, for a while," Chaplin replied, "but then I realized that business was business."

"And when was that?"

"Ten years ago. I've been nursing this place along since then, but last year, when I changed the name and got that painting—in the opposite order—business started to pick up."

"And you're happy now?"

"You said it," Chaplin said. "I wasn't cut out for big business. Jim Wonderly was, and is. End of story."

He went to the other end of the bar to serve drinks. Clint upended the beer mug and finished it off. He turned and saw that the gaming tables had been uncovered and were being set up for business. He decided to forget about other people's business for a while and try to make some money for himself.

SEVEN

When the gaming tables started up the girls came out. They were there to serve drinks, flirt with the men, and make whatever arrangements they wanted to make for when the night was done.

There was a buxom little blonde who caught Clint's eye. He ordered a beer while playing blackjack, just to get her to bring it to him. Normally, he never drank while gambling, but after all, he was only playing blackjack, not poker. He was neither as good at nor as serious about blackjack as he was about poker.

The blonde's name was Doreen, and she began to flirt with Clint, brushing against him as she moved by, even pressing her breasts flat against his back while serving his beer. He was delighted to find that they were not only big, but firm, as well. He wondered if the rest of her was just as full and firm, but he'd lived too many years with his rule against paying for sex to break it now, even for a blonde as cute as Doreen.

He won a bit at blackjack, then abandoned the table for the bar.

Chaplin brought him a beer. "I see you been gettin' along with Doreen."

"We've been doing okay," Clint said.

"She ain't a whore, ya know," Chaplin told him. "She's a flirt, but she ain't for sale."

The bartender had no idea how glad Clint was to hear that. It solved that problem for him.

"That's okay, Chaplin," he said. "I'm not looking for a whore."

"She's a nice girl."

"She seems nice."

"She is," Chaplin said. "I wouldn't want to see her get hurt."

Clint looked at the bartender.

"In what way?"

"In any way," the man said. "Are you one of them slick talkers? Gonna make her think you can take her out of this place?"

"Doesn't she like it here?"

"She likes it, all right," Chaplin said. "I treat all my girls good, but if some man comes along and makes them think he's gonna treat them better—"

"Whoa, Chaplin," Clint said, "back up some. I don't make any promise I'm not going to keep."

"Well," the bartender said, "that's good, that's real good. I'm glad to hear that."

He went to serve some of the other customers and Clint turned, beer in hand, and watched Doreen move around the room. He was imagining what she would look like in some of the items in the Fancy Man store, and that made him smile. A moment later, however, he thought about the three men he'd braced in the store, and the smile went away. Would they come back? Or would their leader come back with other men more suited to the job? And what *was* the job? To scare Banbury into closing—or worse?

He also found the story Chaplin had told him interesting. The man had been a successful businessman at one time, but because of his partner stabbing him in the back when he wasn't looking, he was now a saloon owner—a saloon owner who seemed pretty satisfied with his lot.

And what about James Wonderly? Would he really be so worried about a little store that sold women's underwear that he'd send some men there to rough up the clerk who worked there?

And what about the owner, Andrew B. Robinson, whom Harrison C. Banbury spoke of with such respect? What would he do if he found out what was happening in Kansas City?

Clint was wondering what Banbury was going to do, when Doreen came walking up to him. She was wearing a wrap around her bare shoulders and batted her impossibly blue eyes at him.

"Well?" she said.

"Well what?"

"I'm finished for the night," she said. "Are you coming?"

"Coming where?" he asked, confused.

"Well, to your hotel, of course," she said, and flounced out. He shook his head and hurriedly followed her.

EIGHT

Doreen's breasts were indeed firm, though impossibly large. Even while fondling them, hefting their weight in his hands, Clint wondered how long it would be before they would start to sag. Women of Doreen's type tended to get heavier as they got older; but while she was still in her late twenties, and probably most of her thirties, she would continue to delight men who enjoyed voluptuous women. She had a nice, full, rounded butt to go with those breasts, plump thighs, and a wonderfully soft, smooth-skinned belly that Clint took his time running his tongue over.

She had removed her clothing slowly for him when they reached the room. He'd watched with pleasure and then was surprised when she came to him and began to undress him.

"I like to unwrap my men," she said, "like a Christmas present."

He removed his gun himself, but left the rest of the "unwrapping" to her. When she had him naked she dropped to her knees in front of him and cushioned his semi-erect penis between her pillowy breasts, massaging him there until he was full and hard. Then she took him in her mouth like he was coated with sugar. She was avid, moaning as she suckled him, wetting him thoroughly, taking him deep into her throat and then releasing him just before he could explode.

"No, no," she said, sliding one hand around him, "not yet." She expertly applied pressure, which made his impending explosion subside, then held onto his penis and led him to the bed by it.

On the bed she reclined and allowed him to explore her, which was when he encountered the wonderfully smooth skin of her belly.

"You're not one of those men who likes flat women, I hope," she said. "There's nothing flat about my belly or any other part of me."

"We're in luck," he said. "Tonight I was in the mood for a woman with just the proper amount of meat on her bones."

"Well, you're the one in luck, then." She smiled. "I've got plenty of meat on me. I don't know if it's the proper amount, but there's plenty there."

"Don't worry," he said, sliding his hands beneath her buttocks to cup them and lift her up, "it's the proper amount." And then he buried his face in her blonde muff. . . .

Later, he had his hands on her butt again as she knelt before him on the bed. He took her from behind at her insistence, and had to spread the cheeks of her beautiful ass to do it. Once he was in, though, he released them and moved his hands to her hips. She closed around him and was impossibly tight, and when they started to move he gasped at the amount of friction on him; and then it was a different kind of pleasure as he slid in and out of her, as she pushed her butt back into his belly, taking him all the way in. They moved slowly, because this sort of sex was painful if not done properly. From the sounds she was making, though—moaning, crying out softly, but imploring him on—they were doing it just right. . . .

• • •

Much later it was her face that was buried between his legs, as she sucked him into her hot, wet mouth again, and this time it was plain that she was going to suck him until he was spent. She moaned as she slid his penis in and out of her mouth, down into her throat and out again, her hands caressing him, fondling his balls, stroking his thighs, reaching up to glide over his belly and chest. He watched as her head bobbed up and down, felt the pressure building in his legs and thighs— Jesus, she was sucking it out of him, and when he came it was sudden and intense, and he tried to warn her but couldn't, but it didn't matter because when he did explode she took it all in and sucked more out of him until his hips and butt were up off the bed and then she was laughing, an odd sensation while he was still in her mouth. . . .

They lay together on the bed, both spent, both gasping to catch their breath, her head on his belly, her hand toying with him.

"That," she said, "was incredible."

"I couldn't have put it better myself."

"But I knew it would be as soon as you walked into the saloon," she went on.

"How did you know that?"

"Oh, there's something about the way a man carries himself," she said. "It's a dead giveaway that he's wonderful in bed."

"Really," he said.

"Don't you find that true of women?"

"As a matter of fact, I do," he replied, "but I never really thought about it before."

"I'll bet that once you decided to bed a woman, you've never been disappointed."

"No, I haven't," he said, and then added, "especially not tonight."

"And tonight," she said, rolling over and flicking her tongue over him, "is far from over . . ."

NINE

"Chappy told you what?"

"That I better not hurt you."

"Like how?"

"By making promises I won't keep."

"Like what?"

"Like to take you out of here," Clint said, "away from all this."

"But I don't want to be taken away from all this," Doreen said. "I like Kansas City, and my life."

"I guess he just has a fatherly concern for you and the other girls."

Doreen laughed. "I don't think Chappy has a fatherly concern for any of us. He sleeps regularly with Maria, and sometimes with Loretta, and tries with every girl he hires."

"With you?"

"He tried," she said, "but he's not my type. He doesn't have the walk."

Early sunlight was streaming through his window, and he really couldn't remember if he'd gotten any sleep or not. The night seemed to have been filled with the smell of her, the texture of her skin, and the wetness of her. There didn't seem to have been many quiet, nonfrenzied moments.

Abruptly she swung her legs around, planted her feet on

the floor, and stood up. He watched as she scratched an itch on the inside of one thigh, admiring the line of her back, following it down until it disappeared between her plump buttocks.

"I can feel your eyes on me," she said.

"Where are you going?"

She looked at him over her shoulder, tousled blond hair hanging down over her forehead.

"A girl's gotta get some sleep."

"So come back to bed and sleep."

"No, no," she said. "I get the feeling a girl doesn't get much sleep being in bed with you."

"It seems to me you weren't very interested in me getting any sleep, either."

"That's what I mean," she said, looking around for her clothes. "You bring it out in a girl."

She found her dress and bent over to pick it up. There was not much sway or hang to her firm breasts as she did so. Maybe she wouldn't be one of those women who slid into fat as she got older. Her body seemed incredibly ripe and firm, her breasts and buttocks looking as though they'd burst if he bit into them hard enough.

He got his usual enjoyment from watching her dress. She walked to the mirror above the chest of drawers and gave herself a critical look.

"Can't do a thing about my hair," she said.

"You look beautiful."

She gave him a big smile. "You're a wonderful liar."

"I'm not lying."

She turned, put her hands on her hips, and gave him a critical appraisal.

"Hmm," she said, "maybe you're not."

She walked to the bed and leaned over to kiss him. He pulled her down into a seated position.

"I have to go," she protested.

"I have a couple of questions for you."

"About what?"

"A store in town."

"Yes," she said.

"Yes, what?"

"Yes I'd love to have one of those flimsy, naughty-looking things in the window of the Fancy Man."

"How did you know I was going to ask you about that store?"

"What other store is there in town that would inspire questions?" she asked.

"What do the other girls think of it?"

"They love it."

"Have any of you been in there to buy something?"

"Oh, no."

"Why not?"

"The store hasn't been accepted by the rest of the town," she said. "If we were seen in there . . . well, it might hurt business. Chappy doesn't want us going in there—not yet, anyway."

"When, then?"

She shrugged her smooth, pale shoulders. "As soon as someone breaks the ice, I guess." She stood up and said, "Gotta go. You gonna be around town a while?"

"A few days."

"Well, you know where I am."

"I'll be there tonight."

She walked to the door, turned, and said, "Don't make any promises you can't keep."

"I'll remember."

She opened the door and was gone.

He intended to get up and start the day, but instead he rolled over onto his stomach. He could smell her on the sheets and the pillow—and on himself—and the next thing he knew he was waking up again three hours later, hungry for breakfast. . . .

TEN

At breakfast Clint was interrupted by a man with a badge. This had happened to him time and again. If they didn't catch him at a meal, they caught him in a bathtub. Fact was, after breakfast he had intended to stop in and see the lawman, announcing his presence in Kansas City. This would save him the trouble.

"Clint Adams?" the lawman asked, stopping in front of Clint's table.

"That's right, Sheriff."

"Name's Dan Atkins," the man said. "Mind if I sit a minute?"

"Go ahead," Clint said. "Help yourself to coffee. I always keep an extra cup on the table."

"That's right nice of you," Atkins said, and poured himself a cup.

"What can I do for you, Sheriff?"

"Word gets around, Mr. Adams. I heard you were in town, thought I'd come and pay my respects."

"Are you sure you weren't just coming over to do your job?"

"Well," Atkins said, around his cup of coffee, "that, too." He was in his forties, and didn't seem at all intimidated by Clint's reputation. "I *was* hopin' you'd be able to avoid trouble while you were here."

"I think you're a day late and a dollar short, Sheriff," Clint said.

"Oh? Why's that?"

Clint explained about his run-in with the three men at the Fancy Man. Atkins listened, rubbing his jaw pensively.

"Can't say I recognize two of them, but the third's probably Les Revere."

"Who's he work for?"

"Whoever's paying."

"Do you know who's paying him these days?"

"I can try to find out."

"Did Banbury, the clerk from the store, come in and see you about it?"

"No," Atkins said, "I can't say that he did."

"Why wouldn't he?"

"Maybe he just doesn't want any more trouble."

"More than he had yesterday, or are we talking about trouble he's had before?"

"Well, that store ain't exactly a welcome addition to the town," Atkins said.

"And why's that?"

"Well . . . you were there. You see what he sells. The God-fearing people of this town don't approve of putting ladies' underwear in the window of a store."

"Don't the God-fearing women of this town wear underwear?" Clint asked.

"Well, of course," Atkins said, "but not out where everybody can see."

"So what happened when he opened the store?"

"There was some protest," Atkins replied. "Some of the women in town painted signs and marched in front of his store, but they were so scandalized by what was in the window they had to stop."

"I see," Clint said. "And what about the men in town? Are they scandalized, too?"

"What do you think?"

"Are you a married man, Sheriff?"

"Nope, can't say as I am."

"Well," Clint said, "I think maybe the married men in town aren't as scandalized as they want their wives to think they are."

"You might be right about that, Mr. Adams," Atkins said. "All I know is, I don't think he's sold any merchandise in that store since the day he opened, but he's still there. Maybe people are getting tired of waiting for him to go out of business."

"So they're going to give him a little help?" Clint asked. "Like Revere and his friends, yesterday?"

"Maybe."

"And where do you stand, Sheriff?" Clint asked. "Do you want him to close bad enough to look the other way?"

Atkins's jaw stiffened and he set his coffee cup down.

"I do my job, Mr. Adams," he said, standing up, "as you reminded me when I first sat down."

"I didn't mean to offend you, Sheriff."

"Well, sir," the man said, "you succeeded anyway. Good day."

The lawman turned and left, and Clint managed not to feel too bad about insulting the man. He often found that the times when people protested too much was when they were really dirty—especially men who wore a badge for a living. It was real easy—and tempting—to make some extra money when you spent your entire day toiling behind a tin star.

He turned his attention back to finishing his breakfast.

Sheriff Dan Atkins went directly back to his office after leaving Clint in the hotel dining room. As he entered he saw Les Revere sitting behind his desk.

Revere had done as he'd been told by James Wonderly. He'd found out that Clint Adams was indeed in town and also found the hotel he was staying at. After that he'd decided to send Sheriff Atkins to see how long the Gunsmith would be in town.

"What did you find out?" Revere asked.

"Not much," Atkins replied.

"Is he working for the Fancy Man?"

"I don't know."

"How long is he gonna be in town?"

"I don't know that, either."

"What *do* you know?"

"He seems to be real interested in what's going on at the Fancy Man."

"I already knew that," Revere said in exasperation. "Jesus, Dan, I gave you an easy job to do. Mr. Wonderly's not gonna like this."

"Well, I had to leave abruptly."

"Why?"

"He—kinda insulted me."

"How?"

"He hinted around that I might be, well, for sale."

Revere leaned forward.

"Here's some news for you, Dan: you are!"

"But I couldn't let *him* know that," Atkins said. "I had to act angry."

Revere stood up, shaking his head.

"I guess I'll just have to find out what I want to know by myself."

"How are you gonna do that?" Atkins asked.

"The same way you were supposed to," Revere said, as he walked to the door. "I'm gonna ask him."

ELEVEN

Clint was walking out the front door of the hotel as another man started coming in. They collided, both bounced back a few feet, then stopped and looked at each other.

"Well, well," Les Revere said, with a smile, "if it ain't the ladies' underwear lover."

Clint gave the man a smile of his own.

"If you don't like ladies' underwear," he said, "then there might be something wrong with you."

Revere lost his smile.

"Hey, friend, I like it fine, but on a lady, not in a window."

"I doubt you've ever seen it on a lady, *friend*," Clint said. "Revere, isn't it? Les Revere?"

Revere looked surprised. Sheriff Atkins had a big mouth. He decided to go on the offensive. "You're Adams, right? Clint Adams?"

"My name's Adams," Clint confirmed.

"What would a big-rep man like you be doin' workin' for the fancy dan who runs the Fancy Man?" Revere asked.

Clint doubted that the man even had an inkling that his remark had a rhyme to it.

"What do you mean, working for him?"

"Well, you ain't gonna be clerkin' in his store," Revere said.

Clint laughed aloud this time.

"You think I hired my gun out to a ladies' underwear store?"

"What were you doin' there, then?"

"Shopping for your sister," Clint said.

Revere got red in the face and took a step forward. Clint figured if he'd said "mother" somebody'd be lying dead right then.

"Watch your mouth, mister," Revere said. "Rep or no rep, I'll try you."

"And you'd lose, Revere," Clint said, "so don't even think about it—and as far as your beef with the Fancy Man, forget that, too."

"Why? If you ain't workin' for him?"

"I don't have to be working for him to help him out," Clint said. "I'm in favor of free enterprise."

"Huh?"

"I think he should be able to run his store if he wants to, so tell your boss not to bother sending you around anymore."

"My boss?"

"Yeah, whoever sent you over there to rough him up. I hear there's a fella in town named Wonderly who might fit the bill."

Jesus, Revere thought, *what the hell did that stupid lawman tell him?*

"I ain't got a boss, Adams," he said. "I'm on my own."

"Sure," Clint said. "You just don't like ladies' underwear stores. Well, I'll step aside and let you finish your business in the hotel—or was this your business?"

"Huh?" Revere said, again.

"I guess you'd like to know how long I'm staying in town, huh? Well, to tell you the truth, I'm not all that sure, so we'll all just have you wait and see—you, me, and your boss."

"I told you—"

"Right, right," Clint interrupted, "you don't have a boss. I heard you the first time."

With that Clint stepped around Revere and walked away from the hotel, leaving a very confused man in his wake.

Revere slammed the door of the sheriff's office open so hard Atkins jumped out of his seat.

"Jesus, Les!" he snapped. "You scared the shit out of me."

Revere approached the desk and grabbed the lawman by the front of the shirt.

"What the hell did you tell him?" he demanded, spittle flying into Atkins's face.

"What? Tell who?"

"What did you tell Adams?"

"I didn't tell him nothin'! I swear."

"He knew my name," Revere said, "and he knew Wonderly's name."

"He didn't get it from me," Atkins lied. He may have given Clint Adams Revere's name, but there was no way he'd ever admit it.

Abruptly, Revere released the man's shirt and stepped back from the desk.

"If he didn't hear it from you," he said to Atkins, "then where did he hear it?"

"I don't know about you," Atkins said, "but Wonderly is a well-known name in Kansas City. He could have heard it anywhere."

Revere had to give him that.

"You keep an eye on him," he ordered, "and don't say nothin' to him. Understand?"

"Sure, Les, sure," Atkins said. "I understand."

Revere left the sheriff's office and went to see James Wonderly.

TWELVE

Wonderly listened silently as Revere relayed what had happened that morning, making a small change here and there so that he came out sounding fine and any blame that needed to be laid was laid at the feet of Sheriff Atkins.

But—to his disappointment—all his covering up was for nothing because Wonderly was not interested in affixing blame.

"So, we know the Gunsmith is in town," Wonderly said, "but he claims not to be working for the Fancy Man."

"Right."

"I know I'm right," Wonderly snapped. "Just keep quiet a moment."

"Um . . ." Revere said, then kept quiet while Wonderly worked it out for himself out loud.

"He *claims* not to be working for them, yet he was there to stop you yesterday."

Revere started to respond, then thought better of it and kept silent.

"It doesn't figure that he'd be here by coincidence," the wealthy man continued, "but it also doesn't figure that a man of his reputation would hire his gun out in this fashion."

There was a moment of silence and then Wonderly asked, ''Well, does it?''

Apparently, the man wanted an answer, this time.

''Uh, no, sir, it doesn't,'' Revere said, ''unless . . .''

''Unless what, man? Come on, spit it out!''

''Well . . . unless he's fallen on hard times,'' Revere said. ''I mean, ain't you the one who's always talkin' about progress? About the day of the cowboy comin' to an end? What about the day of the gunman?''

Wonderly stared at Revere for a few moments, then shook his head.

''My God, Revere, maybe you're not as dumb as I think,'' he said.

Revere frowned.

''That must be it,'' Wonderly continued. ''He needs the money badly enough to take the job. Do you know what that means?''

Revere hesitated, then said, ''What?''

''That he'll take a better offer.''

''Oh.''

''Wouldn't he?''

''Sure,'' Revere said, ''I guess.''

''And if he doesn't accept a better offer,'' Wonderly went on, ''then he's into this for an entirely different reason.''

''What?''

''I don't know. First let's see if he takes the offer, and then we'll wonder about that.''

''So . . . you want me to make an offer?''

''Of course not,'' Wonderly said. ''I'll take care of that myself.''

''Oh.''

''Where is he staying?''

''The Kansas House.''

Wonderly stroked his jaw and then said, ''I'll invite him to dine with me at Joe Bassett's Marble Hall.''

Revere frowned again. He'd never been to the Marble Hall.

"What should I do?"

"Hmm?" Wonderly had almost forgotten Revere was there. "Oh, you. Find yourself two or three men you can trust, who can use a gun. We'll need a last resort to fall back on."

"Okay."

"So go now," Wonderly said, waving Revere away. "I've got some thinking to do."

"What about Atkins?"

"What about him?"

"Well, he may have given Adams your name."

"Preposterous!" Wonderly snorted. "The man is too afraid of me."

"Well then, maybe he gave him mine."

"That's of no concern to me." Wonderly said. "That's between you and him."

Revere hesitated, but once again Wonderly seemed to have forgotten he was there. He turned and left.

Ten minutes later James Wonderly stepped to his office door and addressed his secretary, the delicious Eileen Wilson.

"Miss Wilson."

"Yes, sir?"

"Send word to the Marble Hall that I will be dining there tonight."

"Yes, sir."

"And I'll have a guest."

"One guest, sir?"

"Yes, just one."

"All right, Mr. Wonderly," she said. "I'll see to it."

"Yes," Wonderly said, "I know you will."

He lingered a moment, admiring the way she filled out her clothes, firm of hip and bosom, and then withdrew into his office, closing the door behind him. She was so tempting, but she was to be saved for later, to linger over, savor, and enjoy.

Another time.

THIRTEEN

When Clint received the invitation it didn't surprise him. Men like James Wonderly thought their money could buy anything. Well, he'd let Wonderly buy him a meal, but that was all the man's money would get him.

The invitation was left for him at the front desk of the Kansas House hotel, and it very much impressed the young desk clerk.

"Wow," he said, after he'd given Clint the message, "Joe Bassett's Marble House. I've never been there, have you?"

"As a matter of fact, I have," Clint said. Fact of the matter was he knew Joe Bassett, and it occurred to him to go over to the combination saloon, restaurant, and gaming establishment and talk to Joe right away. "Did Mr. Wonderly make arrangements for me to send him an answer?"

"No, sir," the clerk said, frowning. "Why? Would you say no?"

"I might," Clint replied, "but not in this instance. Anyway, thanks for taking the message."

"Sure," the clerk said, still frowning over why anyone would say no to an invitation from James Wonderly.

• • •

Clint caught Joe Bassett having lunch; since it was still several hours from opening time, Clint had to knock several times before the front door was opened by Bassett's head bartender, Jack Kern.

"Clint Adams," Kern said. "What are you doin' in Kansas City?"

"Last time I was here it was just for a blink of an eye, Kern," Clint replied. "Thought I'd stop back in and see how the place had changed."

"It's changed and how," Kern said. "Come on in. Joe'll be glad to see you."

Kern led Clint back into the restaurant, where Bassett was sitting alone at a table. All the other tables had the chairs stacked up on them.

"Look what drifted into town, Boss," Kern said. He and Bassett had been together for years, almost partners, certainly friends, and yet he always called the man "Boss" to his face.

"Clint Adams," Bassett said, standing up to shake hands.

"Stay where you are, Joe," Clint said. "Didn't want to interrupt your meal."

"You're not interruptin' it," Bassett said, "you're joinin' me. Jack, get another chair."

Kern pulled a chair down from atop one of the tables and set it down across from Bassett. Clint sat down. Bassett had put on some weight since he'd last seen him, but if the steak and vegetable plate he had in front of him was his regular lunch, Clint could see why.

"What'll ya have, Clint?" Kern asked.

"I'll just have some coffee, Jack."

"Ya sure?" Bassett asked. "I could have the cook rustle you up a steak. Best steaks in town."

"I don't doubt it, Joe," Clint said. "In fact, I'll be eating here later tonight."

"Is that a fact? Got a lady you want to impress?" Bassett asked.

"No. I've been invited to eat here as the guest of James Wonderly."

Bassett dropped his knife and fork in the act of cutting his steak.

"You're gonna ruin my meal with that kind of talk," he said.

"What's wrong with Wonderly?"

"What ain't wrong with him?" Bassett picked up his utensils again. Apparently, even Wonderly couldn't ruin his appetite for very long. "What's your business with him, Clint?"

"I think he's going to offer me some money."

"To do what?"

"Well . . . nothing, actually."

"How much money is nothing worth these days?" Bassett asked.

"I don't know," Clint said, and then went on to explain what he'd meant. By the time he was done Kern had returned with the coffee, had heard most of the story, and was laughing along with Bassett.

"Leave it to you to get involved with a lost cause like the Fancy Man," Bassett said.

"Is it? A lost cause, I mean?"

"That store hasn't made a sale since it opened," Bassett said. "What would you call it?"

"A slow starter?"

"That's optimistic of you," Kern said.

"I'd've thought you would have bought your girls some stuff by now," Clint said.

"I buy my girls plenty of stuff," Bassett said, "most of it from New York."

"Don't you think they'd like something from the Fancy Man?"

Bassett stared across the table at Clint.

"You got a piece of that place, Clint?"

"No," Clint said, "I just don't like seeing somebody get squeezed, Joe."

"That sounds like you," Bassett said. "What do you want us to do?"

"I just thought maybe you'd tell me something about Wonderly. So you think he'd send some men over to the store to scare a man like Banbury?"

"Wonderly would do anything he thought he needed to do if it would make him some money."

"Sounds like a lot of businessmen I know," Clint pointed out.

"Most businessmen have a line they won't cross," Bassett said, gesturing with his knife.

"And Wonderly doesn't?"

"If he ever did," Kern said, "it blurred a long time ago."

"What if he offers you a bundle, Clint?" Bassett asked. "And I mean an absolute bundle. He's got it to throw around."

"I'm not for sale, Joe," Clint said. "Never have been, never will be."

"That's what I thought," Bassett said. "I was just checking. Well, do you want any special treatment tonight? Maybe we can let Mr. Wonderly know that you're more welcome here than he is."

Clint almost said no, then had a second thought. Wonderly was probably taking him to the Marble Hall to try to impress him.

"You know, Joe." he said slowly, "that doesn't sound like a bad idea. . . ."

FOURTEEN

After leaving Joe Bassett's place, Clint walked over to the Fancy Man. As he entered, Harrison C. Banbury looked up from the counter, appearing frightened for a moment until he recognized Clint.

"Ah, Mr. Adams," the man said, obviously relieved. "How nice to see you again."

"Mr. Banbury."

"Please," Banbury said, "call me Harrison. After all, you did save my life yesterday."

"Well," Clint said, "maybe I saved you some difficulty. Why don't you just call me Clint?"

"Very well," Banbury said, "Clint . . . but I truly think those men might have killed me."

"If you really think that, Harrison," Clint asked, "why would you still be here today?"

"Mr. Andrew Robinson has put this store in my care. I wouldn't be very responsible if I ran away from it, would I?"

"No, but you'd be alive."

"But I am alive."

"Admit it, Harrison," Clint said. "When I walked in you thought it might be those men coming back."

"Yes, I did," Banbury said, "but I took your advice to heart."

"What advice was that?"

Banbury reached underneath his counter and came up holding an over-and-under Greener shotgun.

"You see," he said, "I was afraid I would have to use this. That must have been what you saw on my face."

"Makes sense," Clint said. "Could you, uh, put that away? If I remember correctly, you said you weren't very good with guns."

"The man I bought this from," Banbury said, returning it to its place beneath the counter, "said that wouldn't matter, not with a shotgun."

"He was right, especially not in close quarters like this—but it sure would tear the hell out of some of these nice things, not to mention cover them with blood."

"Well, with any luck I won't have to use it."

"Luck may not have anything to do with it."

"What do you mean?"

"I mean I've taken a hand in your fight," Clint said. "I'm in the game."

"Why is that?"

"Well, partially because I had no choice yesterday, and partly because tonight somebody is going to offer me a lot of money to go away."

"Mr. Wonderly?"

Clint nodded. "He's invited me to dinner."

"And you accepted?"

Clint shrugged. "A man has to eat."

"He will most certainly offer you money," Banbury said, "lots of it."

"And I'll turn him down."

"Why?"

Clint told Banbury what he'd told Joe Bassett just a little while before: "I'm not for sale, Harrison."

"At any price?"

"At any price."

"You're a unique man, then," Banbury said.

"Not so unique," Clint argued. "If he offered you money to walk away from this store you wouldn't take it."

"I'd like to think I wouldn't, but doesn't every man have his price?"

"Maybe," Clint said, "but I kind of care where the money comes from, not just how much it is."

"Well, in that we are very much alike, I think," Banbury said.

"Then we're in this together, Harrison."

"I don't know what I've done to deserve your assistance, Clint," Banbury said, extending his hand, "but I'm very grateful for it."

The two men shook hands.

"I'm sure when I telegraph Mr. Robinson about your help he'll authorize me to pay you something."

"Let's not talk money, Harrison," Clint said. "That's not what this is about."

"All right," Banbury agreed.

"Listen," Clint said, "I'm friends with Joe Bassett, who owns the Marble Hall."

"I know who Mr. Bassett is."

"I think I might be able to talk him into buying some of your items for the girls who work for him."

"That would certainly break the ice for us," Banbury agreed, "but wouldn't that be dangerous for him and his position in town?"

"If Joe agrees he's not going to worry about that. Why don't I come and see you tomorrow morning and I'll tell you all about how my dinner went."

"That would be excellent," Banbury said. "I'll be sure to have a fresh pot of coffee ready."

"I'll be by first thing when you open, Harrison," Clint promised.

"I'll be waiting."

Clint nodded, shook hands once again with the man, and left, not knowing that it was the last time he would ever see Harrison C. Banbury alive.

FIFTEEN

Clint arrived at the Marble Hall early, waiting across the street until he saw a man arrive in an expensive buggy. He'd been brought by a driver, and fit the description given Clint by Joe Bassett and Jack Kern. He waited for the man to enter, gave him ten minutes to be seated, and then went in.

The show was on.

Clint entered the restaurant and stopped just inside the doorway. He looked around and spotted James Wonderly, seated at a large, centrally located table. From it, Wonderly could see and be seen by everyone.

Jack Kern approached Clint and hugged him, as if he hadn't seen him in years.

"What are you doing here?" he asked, loudly enough for everyone to hear him.

"I'm meeting someone," Clint said, looking directly at Kern. "Someone named James Wonderly. Know him?"

"Oh, yes, I know Mr. Wonderly very well," Kern said. "He's a regular guest here, but . . ." Kern turned. Wonderly had been watching and listening to the scene with great interest. ". . . he's seated at his usual table, in the center of the room."

"Won't do," Clint said.

"I realize that," Kern replied. "I'll take you to your regular table, Mr. Adams."

Clint didn't have a regular table at Joe Bassett's, but saying he did was part of the show.

"Please, follow me . . ." Kern said, looking concerned.

He took Clint to a corner table and held out his chair for him—a chair that put his back to a wall. From this chair he could see the whole room.

"I'll talk to Mr. Wonderly," Kern said.

"Do that," Clint replied.

Kern walked to Wonderly's table and said, apologetically, "Mr. Wonderly, your dinner companion has arrived."

"I think the whole room was able to see that, Kern," Wonderly said. "Mr. Adams is to be my guest, not my companion. Bring him to my table, at once."

"I'm sorry, sir, but Mr. Adams maintains a regular table here, which he uses when he's in town."

"That's preposterous," Wonderly said. "I've never seen the man here."

"He's here rarely," Kern admitted, "but sir, he can't sit in the center of the room the way you do."

"Why not?"

Kern leaned over and said in a low voice, "He doesn't want to be shot in the back. If I bring him to your table, sir, there's a possibility you could be hit by a stray bullet."

Wonderly seemed to take this under consideration while Kern stood by with a grave look of concern on his face.

"Mr. Adams would like you to join him at his table, sir," Kern finally said, "if you would."

Wonderly thought it over some more, then stood up and threw his napkin down on the table.

"Oh, very well," he said. "Bring my drink."

"Yes, sir." Kern picked up the glass of champagne Wonderly had ordered. "I'll bring it right along, sir."

Wonderly walked over to Clint's table, and Clint rose to greet him.

"Mr. Wonderly?"

"That's right."

"Clint Adams," Clint said, extending his hand. "I'm sorry about the thing with the tables."

"Very irregular," Wonderly said.

"So is a bullet in the back, Mr. Wonderly," Clint pointed out.

Wonderly cleared his throat. "Yes, well, I suppose so."

"Please," Clint said, "have a seat and we can order."

Kern placed Wonderly's champagne at his elbow and said, "Gentlemen, I'll send over your waiter," adding to Clint, "your regular waiter, Mr. Adams."

SIXTEEN

"You hardly ever come here, and you have a regular waiter?" Wonderly was astonished.

"One I know won't pull out a gun and shoot me," Clint said. "That's an important quality in a waiter, don't you think?"

"I suppose."

"When you invited me here," Clint went on, "it wasn't your impression that I'd never been here before, was it?"

"Well," Wonderly said, "I didn't think—I mean, I didn't know . . ."

"Joe Bassett and I have been friends a long time, Mr. Wonderly," Clint said. "I was very pleased when you chose this place to meet."

"Yes, well . . . I like the food."

"So do I," Clint said. The waiter appeared. "The usual, Mr. Adams?"

"That's fine, Frank."

"Mr. Wonderly?" the waiter asked.

"I'll have the usual."

"And that would be . . . sir?"

"Pot roast," Wonderly said through clenched teeth.

"Very good, sir. Beer for you, Mr. Adams?"

"Yes, definitely."

"And for you, Mr. Wonderly?"

"Wine," he replied, "red wine."

"Yes, sir," the man said. "I'll be back with the drinks, gentlemen."

"The service is also excellent," Clint said.

"Usually," Wonderly said.

Before either of them could say anything else, though, Joe Bassett put in an appearance at their table. He was wearing a black suit and tie and a white shirt, looking every inch the gambler.

"Clint, so good to see you!"

Clint stood up, and he and Joe Bassett shook hands warmly.

"And Mr. Wonderly," Bassett said. "Pleasure to have you back with us, sir. You don't come by nearly often enough to suit us."

"Not often enough to have my own waiter," Wonderly muttered.

"What was that?"

"Nothing."

"If you gentlemen need anything at all please ask for me."

"We will," Clint said.

The waiter appeared with their drinks as Bassett walked off, set them down, and faded away like a good waiter should.

"Well," Clint said, picking up his beer glass, "here's to excellence in all things."

"I'll drink to that," Wonderly said.

"Now," Clint said, putting his beer down, "what was it you wanted to see me about, Mr. Wonderly?"

"I wanted to make you an offer, sir."

"What kind of offer?"

"Er, well, sort of like a job offer."

"Sort of?"

"Well, you wouldn't have to do much."

"What *would* I have to do?"

"Well, actually," Wonderly said, "nothing."

"And for this you would pay me?"

"Handsomely."

"If you don't mind me saying so, Mr. Wonderly," Clint said, "it sounds pretty fishy to me."

"Allow me to explain."

"I wish you would."

"Ten thousand dollars."

Obviously, the amount was meant to impress him. It didn't.

"Mr. Wonderly," Clint said, "the amount doesn't matter quite as much as the job itself."

"I understand you have some connection to the store in town called the Fancy Man."

"You understand wrong, then."

"Excuse me?"

"I'm not connected to that store at all."

"But I understood—"

"—wrong, as I told you."

"But you've been there."

"Oh, yes," Clint admitted. "I quite like the store, actually."

"Which puts you in the minority, I'm afraid."

"Does it?"

"I'm afraid so."

"Well," Clint said, "that's not something that's ever bothered me before."

"I understood there was some trouble there and you, ah, stepped in?"

"Well, now you understand something correctly," Clint said. "Three drunken cowboys were going to bust up the shop—and probably the clerk, as well. I was obliged to stop them. Is that what makes you think I'm connected to it?" Clint laughed, because he thought it would annoy James Wonderly. "Do you think I would hire my gun out to a lingerie shop?"

"Well—"

"I think I see what's going on here, Mr. Wonderly."

"You do?"

"Yes. You think the Fancy Man is going to be a success, and you don't want it to be—not without owning a piece of it."

"That's ridiculous. That store will not be around in a few months."

"I beg to differ," Clint said. "I think that store will be a smashing success within the next couple of months. Mark my words. You heard it here first."

"Why do you say that, Mr. Adams?"

"Because," Clint pointed out, "women wear underwear. It's that simple."

"Are you a businessman?"

Clint laughed again.

"You know what kind of business I'm in—or what kind you think I'm in—or you wouldn't have invited me here to try to pay me off."

"Is that what I'm doing?" Wonderly asked. "I thought I was offering you a job."

"To do nothing."

"That's right."

"For ten thousand dollars."

"You've been listening."

"In my book," Clint said, "that's a payoff. I don't take payoffs, Mr. Wonderly." He stood up.

"You're leaving?" Wonderly could not believe his eyes.

"That's right."

"But the food . . ."

"If I ate it," Clint said, "that would be a sort of payoff."

"You're serious about this?"

"Very."

"You're turning down ten thousand dollars?" Wonderly was totally confused. Men with money always thought other people wanted it.

"Ten, fifteen, fifty," Clint said. "It doesn't matter. I

don't want it.'' He leaned on the table, looming over Wonderly.

''Take my advice,'' he said. ''Leave the Fancy Man alone. Don't send Les Revere or anybody else over there to cause trouble.''

''Or what?'' Wonderly asked.

''There's no 'or what,' '' Clint said. ''It's a simple statement. Don't do it.''

The waiter appeared at Clint's elbow.

''Mr. Adams,'' he said, ''aren't you going to eat?''

''He'll eat both dinners, Frank,'' Clint replied. ''After all, he's paying for them.''

With that Clint left Joe Bassett's Marble Hall, leaving behind a very confused and very angry James Wonderly. Nobody talked to him like that, Wonderly thought. Not even a man with the reputation of the Gunsmith.

Nobody.

Clint Adams was going to learn that.

SEVENTEEN

From Joe Bassett's Clint went directly to the Shady Lady.

"What have you got in the way of food?" he asked Chaplin—or Chappy, as Doreen called him.

"I heard you were eatin' at the Marble Hall with Wonderly."

Clint was surprised. News traveled fast in these parts.

"Where did you hear that?"

"Around," Chappy said. "I've got ears."

"All over town, I guess," Clint said. "Didn't your ears tell you I walked out on him?"

"Him? And a Marble Hall meal?"

"That's right."

"And lots of money, if I know Jim Wonderly."

"You know him better than anyone, I guess."

"I can make some sandwiches, if that'll do you," Chappy said.

"It'll have to."

"Have a seat. Here, take this with you." Chappy drew a cold beer and gave it to Clint.

"Thanks."

Clint carried the beer to a table that suited him, sat, and waited for the sandwiches. When they came they were carried by Doreen.

"You must really be hungry to eat these," she said, putting them in front of him.

"Why? What are they?"

"Egg sandwiches."

"Eggs?"

"Hard-boiled eggs."

Clint took a look at the three sandwiches and said, "They look okay to me."

"Yuck. Why didn't you eat tonight?"

"It's a long story."

"Tell me later?" she asked.

"Definitely."

"Good," she said. "Gotta go to work. See ya."

She ran off, and he picked up the first sandwich, smelled it, and then bit into it. Aside from having a little too much salt, it was fine, and so were the others. He wolfed all three and washed them down with beer.

When he was done he went back to the bar for another beer. There were three bowls of hard-boiled eggs at different points on the bar.

"How were the sandwiches?" Chappy asked.

"Fine," Clint replied. "I'll take another beer."

Chappy brought the beer and said, "There's more eggs on the bar if you're still hungry."

"Salted?" Clint asked, sipping the beer.

"Of course," Chappy said. "I hope they weren't too salty?"

"Nothing another beer won't wash away." Of course the eggs were salty, because Chappy wanted to sell more beer. It was the same in any saloon that provided hard-boiled eggs for their clientele.

"What do I owe you for the sandwiches, Chappy?" Clint asked.

"Forget it," the bartender said. "Doreen looks real happy today. That's payment enough for me."

"You know," Clint said, "your girls could use some new dresses."

"You think so?"

Clint nodded.

"And where do you think I should buy them?"

"Well, I don't know if the Fancy Man carries dresses, but—"

"Oh no," Chappy interrupted. "You're not draggin' me into the middle of *that* fight."

"What fight?"

"The one between the Fancy Man and Jim Wonderly. The one between the Fancy Man and the *whole town*? That fight? Ring a bell?"

"Come on, Chappy," Clint said. "Don't you believe in free enterprise?"

"Sure," Chappy said, "but not when it endangers my business. If I'm caught buyin' stuff from him there's plenty of other saloons in town."

"I thought you'd be more supportive than that."

"Supportive? I don't know the fella who owns that place. I don't even know the man who runs it. For all I know they could be the same man."

Clint realized that was true of himself, as well. He only had Banbury's word that there even was an Andrew Robinson. He decided to check up on both men tomorrow, and he knew just who to send a telegraph message to for help. In fact, there were two men who could—and would—help him, both very good friends of his.

"You've got a point, Chappy," Clint said. "Forget I said anything."

"I mean, I *could* help—"

"Forget it," Clint repeated. "I mean it. I was out of line."

He turned around, caught Doreen's eye, and signaled that he was leaving. She nodded.

"Hey, Clint," Chappy said, "you ain't mad at me, are you?"

"No, Chappy," Clint said, "I'm not mad. I'll see you tomorrow."

"Sure," the bartender said as Clint went out the door, "tomorrow."

EIGHTEEN

Clint woke the next morning with the pleasant warm weight of Doreen on his left arm. He was in no hurry to move her because his right arm—and gun hand—was still free.

He'd gone back to his room the night before to wait for her, and while waiting had thought about the whole Fancy Man situation again. Why was he getting himself involved? Was it because no one else was on the little guy's side? Because once again a man with money was trying to get his way by buying it? Why did that just always rub him the wrong way? Maybe it was because he had friends who had money who didn't have to do that. He had seen men with money make it—and keep it—without crushing somebody else.

Andrew Robinson—whoever he was—had every right to open a store in Kansas City and anywhere else, and everyone who lived there had just as much right not to buy what he was selling. But nobody had the right to bully a man like Harrison Banbury and try to close down Andrew Robinson's business.

There was also the fact that Clint had already promised Banbury that he'd be there to help him, so at this point there was no turning back.

Doreen moaned in her sleep and rolled over onto her

side, releasing Clint's arm. They'd had another night of energetic sex, and he knew she liked to get her sleep in the morning. He decided to get dressed and slip out without waking her. He'd told Banbury he'd be there when he opened in the morning.

He walked the few blocks to the Fancy Man, by his reckoning, five minutes early. When he reached it he looked inside the window, but didn't see anyone. He hadn't asked Banbury where he lived. Maybe he had a room in the back or above the store.

He stood in front of the store and waited ten minutes, ignoring the looks he was getting from people passing by. Finally, he became impatient. The store should have opened already.

He had to admit that he was worried. He was going to have to find some way to get inside and make sure everything was all right.

James Wonderly looked up from his desk as Les Revere entered his office.

"Did you get the job done right this time?" he asked his man.

"It's done."

"What about those extra men I asked you to find?"

"I found them," Revere said. "They're all good men with a gun. They're standing by."

"Hire them."

"Hire them . . . now?"

"Isn't that what I just said?"

Revere kept quiet. He was thinking that the meeting with Clint Adams the night before at the Marble Hall probably hadn't gone so well.

"Yes, sir."

"Go and do it. Now," Wonderly ordered.

"Sure," Revere said. "Uh, how much will you be paying them?"

"Less than I pay you."

"How much less?"

"That's up to you," Wonderly said. "Now go do it."

"Yes, sir."

"One other thing."

"Yeah?"

"Did you change clothes after you were done?"

"Yeah," Revere said. "I had . . . yeah, I went home and changed."

"Well, go wash your face."

"Huh?"

"You've got blood on your cheek."

Revere's hand went to his face, and he said, "Uh, yeah, okay. Uh, thanks."

As Revere left Wonderly sat back in his chair and smiled. Sometime today Clint Adams was going to learn he'd picked the wrong man's business to stick his nose in.

NINETEEN

Clint found his way to the back of the store and somehow wasn't surprised that the back door was unlocked. Even though he was sure that if something had gone wrong it had come and gone, he drew his gun as he entered.

He walked down a hall and found himself facing a stairway that went up. To his left was a doorway that probably led into the store. He decided to go up first.

He discovered Banbury's living quarters above the store. It was small, but expensively furnished. There was a small bar against the wall that featured decanters of what Clint was sure would be fine wines and brandies. Banbury was a man of discerning tastes and he wasn't going to let a little thing like being stuck in the American West keep him from the things he loved. Clint also found a small but select library, with books that included those of Mark Twain and Robert Louis Stevenson—both of whom he had met and admired. Dickens was also present.

In the bedroom was a four-poster bed with a plump feather mattress. The window overlooked the street. Clint looked down, then across at the other windows, and then went back into the other room.

Expensive and comfortable, but there was no sign of trouble up here, so he went back downstairs.

He checked the store, but nothing there had been disturbed. He walked to the front door and checked it again, just in case someone had slipped out the front when he slipped in the back. It was locked.

There was one last place to check. All stores had storerooms. He walked to the back, went behind the counter and through a curtained doorway. Here, in fact, was the storeroom, and among the musty odors of dust and dirt and whatever fragrances the Fancy Man dealt in was an odor that was unmistakable to him.

Blood.

"I found him like that," Clint told Sheriff Atkins, pointing.

"Jesus," Atkins said, looking away. "Somebody worked him over good."

Harrison C. Banbury's face was a bloody mess, and it was obvious that he had been beaten to death by someone who hadn't been careful. There was blood all over the front of his clothes, so whoever had done this must have gotten some on him.

"The front door was locked, the back door was open," Clint said.

Atkins stared at Banbury's body, then turned and left the storeroom. Clint joined him out in the store.

"What are you going to do?" he asked.

"This is beyond me, Adams," Atkins admitted. "I have no experience with this. I throw drunks in jail and break up bar fights. This is murder. I don't know what to do."

"Well, first," Clint began, "you'll have to move the body to the undertaker's. After that, I suggest you call in Federal help if you don't know how to handle this."

"That's a good idea," Atkins said. "I'll get a Federal marshal in here."

"And make sure this place is locked up. Do you have deputies?"

"A couple."

"Have one fetch the undertaker and the other stand guard here."

"Okay," Atkins said, "okay . . . and then what?"

"Well, you might want to talk to anyone who had a motive to kill him."

"Like who?"

"I can think of a couple of people."

"Who?"

"Les Revere and James Wonderly."

Atkins's eyes went wide, and Clint wondered how his first impression of the man as a competent lawman could have been so wrong.

"I can't question them."

"Well then, wait for the marshal to show up. He can do it."

"Wonderly knows the governor."

"What's that got to do with anything?"

"He's an important man."

"Does that mean he can have people killed?"

Atkins was silent. Clint thought that either he didn't have an answer for that, or he did, and the answer was "yes."

"I'm going to get out of here," Clint said. "You have a lot of work to do."

"What are you gonna do?"

"What you should be doing." Clint started to leave.

"Adams, if you start trouble I'll have to throw you in—"

Clint whirled on the man so fast Atkins actually backed up a few steps.

"Don't start trying to act like a lawman with me now, Atkins!" Clint exploded. "Just stay out of my way. I'll talk to the marshal when he arrives, but you and I have nothing more to say to each other."

With that he turned and walked out of the store the way he had gotten in, by the back door.

TWENTY

Clint was upset by what had happened to Harrison C. Banbury. The day after he had promised his help, the man was killed. That didn't sit well with him, and he was stewing about it as he walked down Broadway, headed for James Wonderly's office.

It was clear to him that Banbury's death was a message from Wonderly to him, probably a direct result of their meeting last night. That made the man's death his fault, and obligated him to do something about it.

When he reached the office, despite his foul mood he was taken aback by the loveliness of Wonderly's secretary. He stopped short, staring at her.

"Can I help you?" she asked.

"Who are you?"

"My name is Eileen Wilson," she said. "I'm Mr. Wonderly's secretary. How can I help you?"

"My name is Clint Adams," he said. "I'd like to see Mr. Wonderly."

"Do you have an appointment?"

"No, but I think he'll see me."

"He usually only sees people by appointment, Mr. Adams," she said. "May I tell him what this is in reference to?"

"He'll know. We had dinner last night. He made me an offer."

"I see." She pushed her chair back and stood up. She was as lovely below the waist as she was above. Her body was firm, her skin smooth and pale, her face classically beautiful. She was the kind of woman who was almost too beautiful—or so beautiful it was painful. "I'll ask Mr. Wonderly if he'll see you."

"Thank you."

She knocked on what was presumably Wonderly's door and entered, closing it behind her. Clint didn't wait. He walked to the door, opened it, and entered.

". . . says he wants to see—" Miss Wilson was saying. She stopped as Clint entered and turned to face him, hands out in front of her. "You can't come—" she started, but Wonderly cut her off.

"It's all right, Miss Wilson," he said. "I'll see Mr. Adams."

She turned to look at her boss.

"It's all right," he repeated. "You can go back to your desk."

As she walked past Clint she gave him the kind of look a teacher gives a pupil she's disappointed in. It pained him to have her look at him that way.

"What's so important, Mr. Adams, that you have to barge into my office? Are you interested in my offer?"

"Harrison Banbury is dead."

"I see," Wonderly drawled. "Well, any man's death is regrettable, but since I don't know who he is . . ."

"Harrison C. Banbury runs—or ran—the Fancy Man store."

"I see."

"Somebody beat him to death early this morning."

"How tragic."

"I think you know who did it."

"How could I—"

"I think you had your man, Revere, do it."

"This kind of talk is libelous—"

"I intend to prove it," Clint went on, "and see that you both pay for it."

"If you persist this way I'll have to have my lawyer—" Wonderly began in a threatening tone.

"Lawyer?" Clint said. "Since when do you do business through lawyers."

"I'm a businessman, Mr. Adams," Wonderly said. "Most of my business is done through lawyers."

"Well, then, you better get a lot of them," Clint warned. "Because it's going to take a hell of a lot of them to keep me off of you."

"These threats—"

"Promises, Wonderly. I've just made some promises I intend to keep." Clint turned and walked out of the office before Wonderly could respond.

"I'm sorry about that," he said to Miss Wilson.

"Sorry?" she asked. "You could have gotten me fired. That was a horrid thing to do."

"Let me make it up to you."

"How could you possibly—"

"Have dinner with me."

"Certainly not!" she said. "I don't even know you."

"We've been introduced—"

"I'll have to ask you to leave, sir," Miss Wilson said.

"Clint."

"Sir!"

Clint could see he wasn't going to get anywhere—not today, anyway.

"All right," he said, "I'm leaving. But we'll see each other again."

"Will you be doing business with Mr. Wonderly?" she asked.

"Not exactly," he said.

"Then why would we see each other?"

"Ask him about it," Clint advised. "He'll explain it to you. As to why we'll see each other . . . well, the answer to that is obvious, don't you think?"

He left her sitting there, puzzled.

TWENTY-ONE

The Federal marshal didn't arrive for a week, and when he did it quickly became apparent to Clint that nothing was going to be done.

He was one of the first people interviewed by the marshal, Ben Sunshine, who was using Sheriff Atkins's office.

"Don't look at me like that," Marshal Sunshine said to Clint after they introduced themselves. "That's my damn name."

"I wasn't going to say anything," Clint said.

"You were thinkin' it, though," Sunshine said. "Damn fool name for a grown man, let alone a lawman."

"Hey," Clint said with a shrug, "a name's a name."

He didn't want to get off on the wrong foot with the man over his name.

"All right, Mr. Adams," Sunshine said. "I want you to know what I know."

"All right."

"I know your reputation, and I know that Sheriff Atkins is an idiot. And I know we've got a dead man on our hands. Other than that, I don't know shit, so why don't you fill me in?"

So Clint told him the story of the Fancy Man and its problems.

"You found the body, right?"

"Right."

"You see anyone else around the store?"

"No."

"Do you know of any witnesses?"

"No."

"Then you can't point the finger at anyone and say they definitely did it."

"No."

"And this store sold what?"

"Ladies' garments."

"Underwear?"

"Yes."

"How did the town feel about this?"

"They weren't happy."

"Why's that?"

"Because these items were generally what you'd see on a woman in a whorehouse, and they were right in the window."

"Sounds pretty sick to me," Sunshine said. He was in his early fifties, and Clint could tell that the tie he was wearing was as much a part of his everyday wardrobe as his badge.

"I wouldn't want my wife seein' that stuff."

"Every woman wears underwear."

Sunshine frowned.

"Watch that kind of talk, Adams," he warned. "Sounds to me like we got a whole town full of suspects for this killing."

"I don't think so," Clint said.

"Well," Sunshine said, "fortunately I'm the one in charge of this investigation, not you."

"So you're not even going to talk to Les Revere?"

"No."

"Or James Wonderly?"

"I wouldn't bother a busy man like Mr. Wonderly with this," Sunshine said.

Clint had the feeling that Marshal Sunshine had come to Kansas City with orders not to bother James Wonderly with anything.

"I see."

"That'll be all, Adams," Sunshine said. "I think I have enough information to make my recommendation."

"And what would that be?" Clint asked, standing.

Without looking up from the desk, the lawman said, "I don't make my reports to you, Mr. Adams. Good day."

Clint left, knowing full well what the marshal's recommendation was going to be.

So it was going to fall to him to do something about the death of Harrison C. Banbury—and hadn't he known that all along?

TWENTY-TWO

"So what are you gonna do about it?" Chappy asked. "What *can* you do?"

Clint had gone from his meeting with the marshal to the Shady Lady. Chappy had opened only moments before so he and Clint were the only ones in the place. The bartender had offered Clint a beer, but he opted instead for coffee.

"I know I can't just let them get away with it," Clint said.

"But how do you really know it was Revere, acting on Wonderly's orders? I mean, why would a man do something so . . . brutal?"

"To send a message."

"To who?"

"To me."

"Why?"

"For turning him down," Clint said. "You know the man, Chappy. Would he do that?"

"I knew the man, Clint," Chappy corrected him, "and the man I knew was ruthless in business, but not a killer."

"Couldn't the man you knew years ago have changed?"

Chappy rubbed his jaw and said, "I honestly don't know."

"Well, I do," Clint said. "I looked into his eyes at the

Marble Hall, and then again at his office. He had his man Revere do it."

"Why not just send him after you?"

"You can't teach a lesson to a dead man."

"That sounds odd," Chappy said, "but it makes sense."

"He may be planning to come after me, though."

"Why do you say that?"

"I've seen a couple of men around town who have the look."

"Maybe they just know who you are and are tryin' to work up the nerve to try you."

"It's happened before," Clint allowed. "That could be it, but . . ."

"But what?"

"But I doubt it."

"Well, if he's importing men to send after you, you better get out of town."

"No," Clint said, "if he's planning on coming after me I have to stay in town."

"What?"

"And wait."

"What if he sends . . . I don't know . . . half a dozen guns after you?"

"I'll have to take my chances."

"A dozen?"

"Then I might need some help."

"Don't look at me," Chappy said. "I'm a saloon owner, not a gunman."

"I wasn't looking at you Chappy, don't worry," Clint said. "I have friends I can call upon."

During the course of the week Clint had sent telegrams to Talbot Roper in Denver and Rick Hartman in Labyrinth, Texas, asking for information about Andrew Robinson.

Both Roper and Hartman had given him the same information. Robinson was rich, had opened a string of Fancy Man stores across the country—and was planning more.

"Wait a minute . . ." he said aloud.

"What?"

"I know what I can do to force Wonderly into a move."

"Why force him?"

"Because then I'm in control." Clint was silent, thinking his plan through.

Finally, Chappy asked, "So what are you going to do?"

"Go into business."

"What business?"

"The Fancy Man business."

"Huh?"

"I'm going to reopen the store."

"A ladies' underwear store?" If Clint didn't know better, he'd've sworn the bartender was shocked.

"That's right."

"What about the owner? What's he gonna think?"

"I don't even know if he's been notified about Banbury's death."

"Who would have notified him?" Chappy pointed out.

"That's a good question," Clint said. "Maybe I should do it right now."

"Now?"

Clint pushed away from the bar and said, "It's as good a time as any."

"And what are you gonna tell him?"

"That Banbury's been killed and he'll need to send someone to run the store if he wants to keep it open."

"I thought you—"

"I'll offer to keep it open until he makes up his mind."

"And what if he decides to close it?"

"Then he'll have to come here and get his merchandise and sell the store," Clint said. "By that time, it should be all over."

As Clint left the saloon Chappy couldn't help wondering if it would "be all over" the way Clint Adams wanted it to be.

TWENTY-THREE

It was the first time Clint had been to the Fancy Man since he found Banbury's corpse. He got in the same way he had then, through the back door, only this time he had to force it. Both front and back were locked, and he was sure that the only key resided with Marshal Sunshine.

He looked around behind the counter for anything that might have Andrew Robinson's address on it. When he didn't find anything there he decided to check Banbury's living quarters upstairs.

That was where he found the address, written in several places, including an envelope. He put the paper in his pocket and descended the staircase, letting himself out the back door.

At the telegraph office he stumbled for a moment over what to say to Robinson. He decided to approach the man as if he and Banbury had been friends—and, indeed, perhaps they had been on their way to that before Banbury's untimely death.

In a few lines he told Robinson that Banbury had been killed and that Robinson needed to make some decisions about his store. He signed his name and put down the name of the hotel he was staying in.

"Will you wait for an answer?" the clerk asked.

"No," Clint said. "I'll be at my hotel. Please send it over there when it comes."

"Yes, sir."

Les Revere was getting restless. The three men he'd sent for had been in town for almost a week now, waiting for the word to go after Clint Adams. He, in turn, was waiting for the word from Wonderly, but it still hadn't come.

The men he'd hired were good with a gun, maybe even good enough to take the Gunsmith if the three of them worked together. Right now, however, they were simply getting paid to hang around town. Revere was sure that Clint Adams had seen them and knew what they were. Still, Wonderly wasn't moving.

On the other hand he was pretty pleased with the outcome of the Federal marshal's investigation into the death of the Fancy Man clerk. In that instance Wonderly knew what he was talking about. . . .

"You don't have to worry, Revere," Wonderly had said. "It's all taken care of."

"But . . . this fella Sunshine is a Federal marshal," he'd protested. "Can you buy him?"

Wonderly had smiled and said, "What do I need with a Federal marshal in my pocket when I have the ear of the governor?"

Revere had not been sure whether or not Wonderly was just bragging, but apparently he knew what he was doing. The marshal had concluded his investigation today and would be leaving tomorrow.

Revere had to admit Wonderly knew his business most of the time. Still, he couldn't help being antsy about Clint Adams. A man like that didn't make promises he didn't intend to keep, and Wonderly had told him of the Gunsmith's promises. As long as Adams was walking around, they were still in danger.

If the word didn't come down soon, Revere just might have to take matters into his own hands.

James Wonderly looked down at Broadway, his hands clasped behind his back. The Fancy Man was closed down, which was what he wanted. Clint Adams was still in town, but after the Federal marshal reported his findings, what harm could Adams do? None, to him, anyway. Maybe he'd go after Revere. After all, they were both men who settled arguments with guns. As for Wonderly himself, he was well beyond the reach of a common gunman like Clint Adams. There might actually be no need to send Revere and his new men after him.

No, at the moment, matters were well in hand. . . .

Clint went back to his room to await a reply from Andrew Robinson. The more he thought about his plan the more he liked it. Reopening the store would drive a thorn right under James Wonderly's nail. The man was sure to make a move then.

And Clint would be waiting.

TWENTY-FOUR

When Andrew Robinson's reply came it surprised Clint. The man was coming to Kansas City and would be there the following day. Apparently he was on a tour of his stores, and the telegram had been forwarded to him.

Clint wondered if Robinson would go along with what he had planned. Of course, he had no way of knowing what kind of man this was, or how he felt about the murder of Harrison Banbury. Had they been friends? Or was Banbury simply an employee? Was his murder of major concern to Robinson, or was this just a minor setback?

James Wonderly reread Clint Adams's telegram, then the reply from Andrew Robinson, the man who owned the Fancy Man store.

"What are you gonna do?" Revere wanted to know. "Is it time to take care of Adams?"

"Do you see what an opportunity this is, Revere?" Wonderly asked.

"To get rid of Adams?"

"No, no, I'm talking about a business opportunity," Wonderly said. "Once this fella Robinson is here I can just buy him out."

"Buy him out?" Revere asked. "What do you mean?"

"I mean buy the Fancy Man stores."

"What?" Revere was puzzled. "But I thought you wanted them closed. I thought nobody was going to buy anything from a store like that. You said it would never succeed—"

"But of course it will succeed," Wonderly interrupted. "That was the whole point!"

"Huh?"

"It can't miss, Revere," Wonderly said. "It's just like Clint Adams said. All women wear underwear. This man Robinson is a genius, and I can't wait to meet him."

"I'm confused."

"That's because you're trying to do something you're not good at."

"What's that?"

"Think," Wonderly said. "Just leave the thinking to me, Revere, and when I make money, you'll make money."

"What about the three men we hired to kill Adams?" Revere asked.

"Just keep paying them," Wonderly said. "We'll keep them around as a last resort. Right now my priority is this man Robinson."

"But he's coming here to see Adams."

"He's got to eat," Wonderly said, "and where would a man of his means eat here in Kansas City?"

"The Marble Hall?"

"Right. And when he does, I'll be there. I'll close my deal before Clint Adams even knows what happened."

"And then what?"

"And then he might as well leave town," Wonderly said, "because I will own the Fancy Man store."

When Les Revere left his boss's office he was still a very confused man.

Since visiting James Wonderly's office Clint had seen his secretary, Eileen Wilson, around town. All heads turned when Miss Wilson walked down the street, but she didn't seem to notice it. She had the kind of grace that comes naturally to few women.

He hadn't approached her, however. He was getting all he could handle from Doreen at night, and he hadn't had time to think about pursuing another woman during the day.

Before Marshal Sunshine left Clint tried to get the keys to the Fancy Man from him.

"I can't do that, Adams," Sunshine said. "You have no right to them."

"Who does?"

"The owner."

"But he's not here."

"Then the keys will remain in the sheriff's office until he shows up."

That was Sunshine's last word on the matter, and he rode out of town the next day—the day before Andrew Robinson was to arrive.

"I have to admit," Doreen said, the morning of Robinson's arrival, "you've already stayed here longer than I expected—not that I'm complaining."

"Longer than I expected, too," Clint said, strapping on his gun belt, "but I'm not complaining, either."

He walked to the bed and kissed her.

"So this fella comin' into town, he's real rich?" she asked.

"Filthy with it."

"Like Wonderly?"

"I don't know how rich Wonderly is," Clint said. He hadn't even thought about the two men's similarities.

"He's filthy with it," Doreen said. "Everybody says so."

"Well, I guess everybody would know better than me," he said. "I have to go. I'll see you later. Sleep here as long as you like."

Doreen had begun staying in Clint's room each day after he left, and today would be no different. He closed the door on her and set off to meet Andrew Robinson at the train station.

TWENTY-FIVE

When Clint got to the train station he was surprised to see Eileen Wilson there. From her reaction, she was surprised to see him, too.

"Hello, Miss Wilson."

"Mr. Adams."

"What brings you here?"

"I might ask you the same thing."

"You might," Clint said, "but the fact is, I asked you first."

"Not that it's any of your affair," she said, "but I'm meeting someone for Mr. Wonderly."

"And who might that someone be?"

"Now I *know* that's none of your affair."

"Could it be Mr. Andrew Robinson, the owner of the Fancy Man store?"

She frowned.

"How do you know that Mr. Robinson owns the Fancy Man?" she demanded.

"Because I sent him a telegram about it," Clint said. "I'm the one who informed him that his man, Banbury, had been killed."

"An awful thing," Eileen Wilson said.

"You wouldn't know anything about that, would you, Miss Wilson?"

"About the man being killed? Heavens, how would I know anything about that?"

"I just thought you might have heard your boss tell Les Revere to kill him."

"I heard no such thing," she said frostily, "because it never happened."

"If you say so," Clint said. "You probably know Revere a lot better than I do. If you say he's not a killer, I'll have to take your word for it."

"I don't know Mr. Revere well at all," she said. "The fact of the matter is I think he's . . . an odious man. It wouldn't surprise me if he was a killer."

"Then you could tell me—"

"But I do know Mr. Wonderly, and he'd never have anyone killed."

"Never?"

"Never."

"That's a long time," Clint said. "Tell me something, Miss Wilson, since we're stuck here waiting for the same train. Just how rich is your boss?"

"He's the richest man in Missouri." She seemed very proud of that fact.

"That rich?"

"And he's earned every penny."

"You sound very much like a secretary who might be in love with her boss, Miss Wilson."

"That's preposterous," she said.

"Why?"

"First of all he's married, and second . . ."

"What's second?"

"I'm not in the least attracted to him."

"Not even to his money?"

"It would take more than money to make me fall in love with a man, Mr. Adams."

"Well, I'm glad to hear that, Miss Wilson. In fact, you

sound like an honest, forthright young lady."

"I like to think I am."

"Then how did you end up working for a skunk like Wonderly?"

"I'll thank you to stop making rude remarks about my boss," she said. "He advertised for a secretary and I replied to the ad. He hired me."

"How long ago?"

"Six months."

"What happened to the secretary he had?"

"She left town . . . suddenly."

"I see."

"You can't draw any negative conclusions from that."

"Oh, I can if I want to."

She glared at him, but before she could say anything they both heard the train whistle.

"I have to meet the train."

"So do I," Clint said. "Mr. Robinson is expecting me. Is he expecting you?"

"No, he is not. I've come to extend an invitation to him from Mr. Wonderly."

"Dinner, no doubt."

"As a matter of fact, yes."

"At the Marble Hall."

"Excuse me."

He allowed her to pass him, but then walked out onto the platform right behind her.

"Tell you what I'll do for you, Miss Wilson."

"And what could you do for me, Mr. Adams?"

"I'll introduce you to Mr. Robinson and allow you to extend your boss's invitation before he and I do our business."

"That's very kind of you."

"Not at all," Clint said. "I find I have to try very hard to get back into your good graces."

"You were never *in* my good graces, Mr. Adams."

Clint smiled and said, "Well, then, I guess I have to try even harder than I thought, don't I?"

TWENTY-SIX

When the train pulled in several people stepped down from it, but only one figured to be Andrew Robinson. It wasn't only the expensive clothes that gave him away, but his demeanor, as well. Clint knew he'd be dealing with a wealthy man. He only hoped that this man's wealth had affected him differently than James Wonderly's had affected him.

"Mr. Robinson?" Clint asked.

Robinson turned to face him. He was tall, well dressed, and barbered, and somewhat younger than Clint had expected. He hardly seemed to be thirty.

"Mr. Adams?"

"That's right."

The two men shook hands, and then Robinson looked at Eileen Wilson. Being wealthy had not affected his ability to appreciate a lovely woman.

"And who have we here?"

"Andrew Robinson, this is Miss Wilson."

"Eileen Wilson," she said, "representing Mr. James Wonderly."

"I don't believe I know the gentleman," Robinson said, "but it is certainly a pleasure to meet you, Miss Wilson." He took her hand and kissed it.

"My employer, Mr. Wonderly, has many holdings in

Kansas City, Mr. Robinson, as well as throughout Missouri and Kansas. He would be very grateful if you would join him for dinner this evening at the Marble Hall, our finest restaurant.''

''Well, it's a generous offer, indeed, Miss Wilson,'' Robinson said, ''but I'm afraid I have some business to discuss with Mr. Adams that might very well run through dinner.''

''That's too bad.''

''However, I'll be free for dinner tomorrow night, if he would like to do it then.''

Eileen Wilson smiled. ''That can be arranged.''

''Excellent,'' Robinson said, taking her hand in both of his. ''And would you be joining us?''

''I don't believe so, Mr. Robinson,'' she said. ''I am rarely present when Mr. Wonderly conducts his business.''

''Too bad,'' he said. ''Well, I hope I will get to see you again, nevertheless.''

''I'm sure you will, sir,'' she said. She looked at Clint, then back at Robinson. ''If you gentlemen will excuse me.''

They both watched with great appreciation as she walked away, and then Robinson said, ''So she works for the son of a bitch who had Banbury killed?''

As a last thought the day before, Clint had sent a telegram to Talbot Roper in Denver, asking him in turn to send a telegram to Andrew Robinson and fill him in. Clint didn't know if Wonderly had a way of seeing incoming and outgoing telegrams, but if he did he hoped that the man would only intercept telegrams to and from Robinson.

''It was clever of you to have Roper telegraph me,'' Robinson said.

Robinson had checked into the Kansas House, and he and Clint were now sitting in the dining room, talking over coffee.

''I'm just taking precautions, which may or may not be necessary,'' Clint said. ''In fact, Wonderly may be reading all my telegrams, but I hope not.''

"Now that I'm here," Robinson said, "why don't you tell me the whole story from start to finish?"

"It won't take long," Clint said, "if I just hit the high spots . . ."

"So you have no proof that Wonderly had Revere—or anyone—kill Banbury."

"No, I don't."

After a moment Robinson said, "Well, I guess the marshal needed proof, but I don't."

"Why not?"

"I know your reputation, Mr. Adams," Robinson said, "but, beyond that, I checked you out thoroughly with . . . well, some mutual acquaintances."

"And how did I come out?"

"You get the blue ribbon. I'll take your word for it that Wonderly and Revere killed Banbury. Now, how do we get them for it?"

"Do you intend to keep the store open?"

"The store is not my top priority," Robinson said. "Finding Harrison's killer is."

"I'm glad to hear that," Clint said, "but I think the way to do that is to keep the store open."

"I'd have to bring someone in to run it."

"Later."

"What do you mean?"

"After we get the killers," Clint said.

"So who will run it in the meantime?"

"Me."

"You? You'd be a storekeeper?"

"Why not?"

"You're not cut out for it."

"I can handle it for a while," Clint said. "There's one other thing you'll have to do, though."

"What's that?"

"Not sell out to Wonderly."

"You're also assuming that's why he wants to buy me dinner?"

"Yes."

"We're thinking along the same lines, Mr. Adams."

"Clint."

"Clint," Robinson said, "I think we're going to get along."

TWENTY-SEVEN

Clint and Andrew Robinson—who was actually thirty-five years old, not the thirty Clint had originally guessed—decided that they had to make Clint's taking over of the Fancy Man very obvious. For this reason they walked over to the sheriff's office together to retrieve the key.

"This looks in order," Sheriff Atkins said, handing Robinson back his identification papers.

"Then may I have the key to my store, please?" Robinson asked.

"Sure," Atkins said. "I guess if you're gonna sell it you'll need the key."

"Who said anything about selling it?"

Handing over the key, Atkins said, "I just assumed, after everything that's happened—"

"Here you go, Clint," Robinson said, giving the key to Clint.

"Uh, why are you giving him the key?" Atkins asked, confused.

"Mr. Adams now works for me."

"You mean—"

"That's right, Sheriff," Clint said, brandishing the key. "I'm reopening the store today."

As they left the sheriff's office Clint was sure that word

would get back to Wonderly. The only question was how fast.

"He *what*?" Wonderly demanded.

Atkins fidgeted in front of Wonderly's desk.

"He hired Adams to run the store."

"That's . . . inane!"

Ben Atkins didn't know what that meant so he kept quiet.

"Clint Adams is a gunman," Wonderly said, "not a shopkeeper."

"I know."

"Then what is the man thinking?"

"I don't know."

"Of course you don't know," Wonderly said. "You're an idiot. Get out!"

Gratefully, Atkins did just that.

Wonderly turned his chair around and stared out the window at the sky. He still had time. Robinson had agreed to dinner the next evening. He was sure he could make the man an offer for his stores that he couldn't afford to refuse. Once the Fancy Man stores were his the first thing he'd do would be to fire Clint Adams.

"Ridiculous!" he snapped.

Clint unlocked the door to the store and entered with Robinson close behind him.

"The merchandise looks like it's intact," Robinson said.

"There was no struggle out here," Clint said. "It all happened in the back room."

"I'd like to see."

"Andrew—"

"Please."

"All right," Clint said, and led the way.

Harrison C. Banbury's blood had seeped into the hard-packed dirt floor, marking the spot where he had been found.

"Jesus," Robinson said, "poor Harry . . ."

He turned and hurried out.

Clint rejoined Robinson in the store.

"What's your plan?" Robinson asked.

"Once you turn down Wonderly's offer he's going to want to close you down—one way or another."

"What's that mean?"

"That means he'll do anything. He's already murdered a man. I wouldn't put it past him to try to burn the place to the ground."

"You can't be around all the time," Robinson said, "and neither can I."

"I can."

"How?"

"By living upstairs, with your permission."

"You have it."

"What were your original plans?"

"Two nights here, at most," Robinson said, "then on to Denver. Should I stay?"

"I don't think so."

"Why?"

"Your life might be in danger."

"Yours definitely will be."

"I know," Clint said, "but I can look after myself a lot easier if I don't have to look after you as well. Go to Denver. I'll contact you there."

"Through Talbot Roper?"

"That's a good idea," Clint said.

"I've used Roper before," Robinson commented. "He's a good man."

"Then stick with him," Clint said. "Wonderly may forget about you once you're out of Kansas City—but then again, he may not."

"Am I safe having dinner with him?"

"I think so. He won't do anything in public. I'll alert my friend, Joe Bassett, who owns the place. He'll have his man, Kern, look after you. After that, I'll put you on the train to Denver day after next, myself."

"So for tonight we're sage?" Robinson asked.

"For the time being," Clint said, "yes."

"Good," Robinson said. "I'd like to get out of here. I can't help thinking of poor Harry . . ."

The man seemed genuinely distraught.

"Come on," Clint said, taking Robinson's arm, "I'll walk you back to the hotel."

TWENTY-EIGHT

Clint moved out of the hotel and into the room above the store thc next morning. Doreen didn't stay with him that night because she didn't feel well, so he got up early and moved his things. He'd tell her about it later, but he'd also have to tell her that she couldn't stay with him anymore. It was too dangerous. If Wonderly sent somebody at night to kill him, Doreen could easily get caught in a cross fire. If Clint was going to look after himself he had to have no one else around him to distract him.

Once Clint was all moved in he went down to the store and looked at it with a new eye. He wanted to know where everything was, so that if anything was out of place he'd know it right away. It would serve as a warning to him that someone was either there or had been there.

When he was satisfied that he knew the place backward and forward he turned the CLOSED sign around so it said OPEN and unlocked the door.

The Fancy Man was open for business again.

Clint got some idea of how lonely Harrison C. Banbury must have been just in that first day. He also learned just how hypocritical the people of Kansas City were. He could see the looks on their faces when they first looked in the windows of the store, before they put on their public faces of outrage for their neighbors. He could see the longing in the faces of the women, the excitement on the faces of the men. What was the big deal, anyway? It was just underwear, after all.

Late in the afternoon he looked up from the counter and saw a woman actually enter the store. He was surprised until he saw it was Doreen—and then he was doubly surprised.

"Doreen," he said, "what are you doing here?"

"What does it look like I'm doing?" she asked. "I'm shopping."

"But . . . aren't you afraid of what people will think?"

"I'm a saloon girl, Clint," Doreen said. "The people are gonna think what they want. Ooh, I like this. Would you like this on me?"

He couldn't even tell exactly what it was, but he knew that he would like it on her.

"Yes."

"Good. I'll try it on." She took it off the rack.

He looked around and said, "Well, I guess you'll have to use the storeroom, only . . ."

"Only that's where poor Mr. Banbury was found?"

He nodded, then said, "Wait here."

He went into the back room, found a piece of canvas, and laid it over the bloody spot of the floor.

"All right," he said, coming back into the store.

"Thank you, Clint," she said. "I just can't wait to see this on me, can you?"

Actually, he couldn't. Ever since he first saw the Fancy Man store and its products he'd been wondering what some of these items would look like on a woman. Now he was going to find out.

"Clint?" Doreen called from the back.

"Yes?"

"Could you come back here for a minute?" she asked. "I'm not sure I have this on right."

He started to say he wouldn't know if it was on right, but instead he just went into the back room. He stopped short when he saw her. Most of her was showing through the gauzy garments, and her opulent breasts were squeezed together and up, so that she was almost spilling out of the top.

His mouth went dry.

"Do you like it?"

The material was black, but see-through, seemed filmy, but was supporting her breasts and squeezing her waist. She did a turn, and he could plainly see the cheeks of her beautiful ass. She wasn't tall, but it almost made her legs seem long.

"I like it very much."

"Show me," she purred. "Come and show me how much you like it."

She put her arms out to him and her breasts almost did come spilling out. He went to her and took her in his arms, kissed her and let his hands roam all over her. He forgot that Banbury had been killed here, forgot that the front door wasn't locked. He found the stays on the thing and peeled it off of her. It had done its job, and now it ended up on the floor, on top of the tarp that was covering Harrison C. Banbury's blood.

Clint pushed Doreen back against some crates, then lifted her up onto them so he could kneel on the floor in front of her, spread her wide open and dive in with his tongue.

"Oooh, yes, oh . . . oh . . . oh yes," she said, wrapping her fingers in his hair as he licked and sucked her. She rested her legs over his shoulders, and he took her weight in his hands by sliding them beneath her and cupping her ass. He continued to feast on her sweetness until suddenly her legs began to jerk uncontrollably and then she cried out as her pleasure took over.

He stood then, dropped his gun belt and pants around his ankles and drove his rigid penis into her. She gasped, her eyes widening, and then she wrapped her legs around his waist and held on for dear life as he pummeled her, pounding in and out of her, keeping his hands beneath her to cushion her butt on the crate. The last thing he wanted was to give her a bunch of splinters.

Finally, he straightened up and lifted her off the crate. All of her weight was in his hands and on his penis. Now, instead of him banging into her she was riding him up and down as hard as she could. His legs began to tremble either from the threat of release or from holding her weight, he didn't know—and didn't care. He found a softer perch for her and set her down on it, and then it was he doing the work again, slamming into her as she moaned and cried out, pulling his hair, scraping his back with her nails, biting his shoulders with her sharp little teeth until once again she was caught in the maelstrom of sensations that was her orgasm. Her breath caught in her throat, her body tensed, and then he exploded inside of her and both of their bodies began to move and shake uncontrollably as he emptied into her, her insides hungrily sucking more and more from him, more than he ever thought he had to give. . . .

TWENTY-NINE

Doreen bought the item—the price was right on it—and the Fancy Man had its first sale. Clint was happy to take credit for that, because if he hadn't been running the store Doreen would never have come in, and when she saw the effect the garment had on him, she bought another one as well.

The next morning he came down and opened the store, having spent the night in the dead man's bed. That didn't bother him, though. Hadn't he had sex practically on the man's grave? He'd explained to Doreen that she couldn't stay with him there because it was dangerous, and he asked her not to come back into the store. He'd been so distracted by her that the place could have burned down around them and he wouldn't have noticed. When he told her that she was very pleased. She told him she'd miss him, but that she'd still be around when this was all over.

He was prepared to have another day by himself—unless Revere and his men decided to come in. He looked out the window and saw one of Revere's men standing across the street. Well, at least he knew where one of them was.

He went to check the back door to be sure it was locked, then decided to stack some crates in front of it so that it wouldn't be easy to force—and if someone did force it, they'd make a hell of a racket.

When he came back into the store he saw that he had a customer, a tall, slender woman with dark hair pulled into a bun. He hadn't heard her come in. He was going to have to install a bell above the door.

"Well, hello," he said.

"Oh!" She jumped slightly and colored, embarassed. She was holding a garment similar to the one Doreen had bought.

"I didn't mean to frighten you," he said. "Can I help you?"

"Well, I . . . I walk past the store so often, I just thought . . . well, who cares what people think, you know? I thought I'd stop in and . . . look."

"Well, I'm glad you did," Clint said. He decided not to question the wisdom of the woman's decision. He might scare her away.

She looked to be about forty-five, but was a handsome woman who would have been lovely if she dressed a bit differently and did something with her hair. Also, she had deep creases in her forehead that didn't belong there. Some man, he thought, had put those there.

"You have many . . . unusual items in your store," she said, looking around.

"To tell you the truth, ma'am, they're just as new to me as they are to you."

"I see. So you wouldn't be able to . . . recommend something?" She was holding the item in her hands close to her breast now.

"Recommend? For what reason?"

"My husband . . . he ignores me, I'm afraid," she said haltingly. "I thought something from here might . . . change that."

"Well," Clint said, "I don't see how any man could ignore you if you were wearing what you've got in your hands."

She looked down at the garment as if she'd forgotten it, then back at Clint.

"Is there someplace I could . . . try it on?"

"Yes, ma'am," Clint replied. "I can let you use our storeroom."

"Thank you, Mr. . . ."

"Adams, ma'am," he said. "Clint Adams. This way."

She followed him to the door of the storeroom, then stopped and looked at him.

"My name is . . . Stella."

"Well, Stella," Clint said, "if you try it on in there you can come out and have a look in the mirror over here."

She looked over at the full-length mirror he was indicating, then nodded and went into the storeroom.

Clint wondered if this was going to start a trend. Doreen yesterday and now Stella today. Maybe if these women had made up their minds earlier poor Harrison Banbury would still be alive.

"Mr. Adams? Clint?"

"Ma'am?"

"Could you help me a moment?"

Clint hesitated, then said, "Help you?"

"Yes, please?"

"Well . . . sure."

He went into the storeroom and saw Stella standing there wearing a very revealing article of Fancy Man underwear. He was surprised at how it made her look. Gone was her schoolmarm-like appearance. She'd let her hair down while trying the item on, and—as with Doreen—it pushed her breasts up, breasts that were surprisingly larger and firmer than he thought. Also, this woman actually did have long legs, and the outfit showed them off to their best advantage.

"Is this on correctly?" she asked, turning for him as Doreen had done.

She had a much smaller ass than Doreen, but it was perfectly shaped, firm and smooth. She had been transformed from the rather drab woman who'd entered the store to this lovely, exciting creature who was more naked than not. In the closeness of the storeroom he could smell her excitement, and it excited him.

"Um, yes, ma'am," Clint said, "it sure looks like it's on right."

She walked up to him and asked, "You don't think my husband could ignore me in this, do you?"

"No, ma'am." Clint had to wet his dry lips. "I'm sure he couldn't."

"Could . . . you ignore me?"

"No, Stella," he said, "I surely couldn't. I don't think any man could."

She smiled then, and it made her much prettier than when she had come in. He wondered how long it had been since she'd smiled that way.

"You're sweet," she said, and kissed him.

Her lips were thin, but soft, although the kiss was firm.

"Stella," he said against her mouth, "your husband . . ."

"Hush," she said, and silenced him by sliding her tongue into his mouth. He put his hands on her firm ass, kneading it, running his hands up and down the backs of her thighs, touching her waist, sliding his hands up to her breasts.

"Um," she said in a whisper—although it might have been "Yum"—"now you can help me get it off . . ."

THIRTY

Clint was surprised at the passion the Fancy Man garments could arouse in both men and women. Here he was with a woman he had only just barely met and he was pulling her clothes off of her, revealing the flesh beneath to be smooth and firm.

Her nipples were incredibly sensitive because as soon as his mouth and tongue touched them she gasped and shuddered. Over the next twenty minutes or so he discovered a woman who had been ignored so long by her husband that her reactions to him and the things they were doing were extreme. Her nipples blossomed, her skin became rosy, her lips swelled from their kisses—how would she explain that tonight?—and when he spread her legs and touched her there she almost cried.

He'd learned from having Doreen in that back room the day before. He found a blanket and spread it on the floor before lowering Stella onto it and then spreading her, like a flower coming to life, so he could literally attack her with tongue and lips and fingers. He stroked her, licked her, and kissed her until she was erupting beneath his touches, and then he stood, moved between her legs and entered her . . .

• • •

"Oh, thank God," she said, later. She was still naked, but no longer embarassed. They were lying side by side on the floor, and Clint once again thought about the place burning down around them. If women were going to start coming in to shop he was going to have to stop letting them try on items.

"Thank God?" he asked.

She propped herself up on an elbow and looked at him. Her lips looked bee-stung, they were so swollen, but the creases that had been in her forehead when he first saw her were gone. She appeared much more relaxed, probably more than she had been in months—or years.

"Thank God I'm still a woman," she said, "that I can still respond to the touch of a man."

"Your husband—"

"Is a bastard," she said. "He brings women to the house."

"He takes them to your bed?"

"We have separate rooms."

"Why don't you leave?"

"He won't let me," she said. "It would . . . embarrass him. He has a reputation to uphold."

"So buying one of these items . . ."

"It was really for me. He'll never see it."

"Maybe," he said, "another man would appreciate it."

"I didn't think so," she told him, "not until today. Thank you." She leaned over and kissed him. "Now I have to get dressed and leave—but not before I buy this wonderful piece of underwear."

They went out front after she had dressed, her hair pinned back up, and she bought the item.

"Stella—"

She put her hand on his.

"Don't say anything, Clint," she said. "We'll probably never see each other again, and I thank you so much for this afternoon."

"I should thank you."

"I don't think so," she said. "Not by a long shot."

She took her purchase and walked to the door, then turned and said, "I'm going to tell all my friends to come here."

As she went out the door he thought he really was going to have to stop letting women try things on in the store. He didn't think he had the strength for it.

THIRTY-ONE

James Wonderly was dressing for his dinner with Andrew Robinson when his wife came in to tell him that someone was there to see him.

"Who is it?"

She made a face and said, "That man Revere."

Wonderly looked at his wife. She looked different today. He hadn't noticed her in some time, but today she seemed to be giving off a different kind of—what was it? Odor?

"What have you done?" he asked.

"About what?" she asked.

"I mean, to yourself. What have you done? Fixed your hair differently. New dress?"

"No," she said with a sigh, "my hair is the same, no new dress."

"Well, something's different," he said, more to himself than to her, but he didn't have time to dwell on it now. "Tell Revere I'll be right down."

"Yes, dear." She turned and left his bedroom.

Wonderly finished buttoning his shirt and slipped on his jacket. The mirror told him he looked every inch the successful businessman he was. The wealthy man from the East would have nothing on him tonight.

He left his bedroom and went down to the living room, where Les Revere was waiting.

"What is it, Revere?" he asked. "I have a dinner meeting to get to."

"Remember I told you Adams had a customer yesterday?" Revere asked.

"Yes, one customer. A saloon girl. So what?"

"He had another one today."

Wonderly turned to look directly at Revere.

"Another one?"

"Yes."

"That's two in two days."

"Yeah." Revere could count, no matter how stupid Wonderly thought he was.

Wonderly scratched his cheek and thought for a moment. What was happening? Were the women of Kansas City starting to realize what he'd known all along, that this store could be a huge source of income?

"Another saloon girl?"

"No," Revere said. "My man didn't know her, but he said she was a respectable woman, not a saloon girl. Older, in her forties. Still looked pretty good, he said. He, uh, also said she was in the store at least as long as the saloon girl the day before. He thought maybe her and Adams were—"

Wonderly cut him off with a chopping motion of one hand.

"I'm not interested in the sordid details," he said. "It seems as if I'm making my offer to Andrew Robinson just at the right time."

"What do you want me to do?"

"Just have your men continue to watch the store," Wonderly ordered.

"Adams knows they're there," Revere pointed out. "He's too good not to."

"That's fine," Wonderly said. "I don't care if he knows."

"Okay. You're the boss."

"Yes, I am. Is my carriage outside yet?"

"I don't know," Revere said. "It wasn't there when I came in."

"Check and see if he's there, will you?"

"Sure."

Wonderly patted his pockets, made sure his wallet was there. Quickly he went over his offer, wondering if—in light of these developments—he should increase it slightly.

Maybe just slightly. After all, he didn't want Robinson to think him too anxious.

THIRTY-TWO

Clint closed the store at six o'clock. Five minutes later he had to unlock the door for Andrew Robinson.

"I just thought I'd stop by on my way to my dinner meeting," Robinson said.

"We had another customer today."

Robinson smiled.

"Two in two days. That's good."

"Does it start that way?" Clint asked. "That slowly, I mean."

"Sometimes," Robinson said. "New York is the only place the store was accepted immediately—oh, and New Orleans."

"You opened one in New Orleans?"

"Just last week. It's already making more money than any of the others, except New York."

"You really came up with a great idea here, Andrew."

"Do you think so?" Robinson seemed pleased by Clint's endorsement.

"I'm no businessman, but it seems that way to me."

"Thanks, I appreciate it," the man said. "I have another idea, as well."

"What's that?"

"I want to do a mail-order catalogue," Robinson explained. "You know, like Sears Roebuck?"

"That sounds like a good idea, too. When will you start that?"

"Oh, not until I've established the stores. The catalogue will have the same name."

"I see."

"What will you be doing tonight?"

"I think I'll just stay upstairs," Clint said. "I want to be near the store."

"I'll come by and see you after dinner to tell you what happened."

"All right, but then you should go straight to your hotel and stay there. I'll come by in the morning to take you to the train station."

"I can get there alone. What if they try something with the store?"

"When you turn down Wonderly's offer tonight I don't think he'll react right away."

"Which means I'm safe to go to the train alone."

"Just do me a favor and let me walk you there."

"All right," Robinson said, "all right. I'll see you in a little while."

"Want some advice?"

"What?"

"Don't turn Wonderly down until after you've eaten," Clint said. "The Marble Hall serves the best steaks in Kansas City."

"I'll keep that in mind."

"Good luck."

"You, too."

Clint let Andrew Robinson out and locked the door behind him. He checked the back door once again, then went into the back room. He could still smell the scent of the sex he and Stella had that afternoon. It aroused him and for a moment he was sorry he had told Doreen not to come over tonight. He shook his head and went upstairs.

Wondering what he was going to do for dinner, he went

to the window and looked out. Across the street was one of Wonderly's—or Revere's—men. He didn't know what the chain of command was, but somebody was out there. In fact, the man was in the doorway of the café that was directly across the street.

Clint went back downstairs and out the front door, locking it behind him, and started across the street.

The man had been lounging, leaning against the wall of the café. When he saw Clint coming over he straightened up and looked both ways, as if undecided what to do. His indecision caused him to be stuck in the doorway when Clint got there.

"Excuse me," Clint said.

"Huh?" the man said. "What?"

"I'd like to get by," Clint said. "I'm hungry, and thought I'd have dinner here."

"Uh . . . oh," the man said, and stepped aside.

"Thank you."

Clint was able to eat dinner and keep an eye on the store. He didn't know where the other man had gone. Probably to another doorway.

THIRTY-THREE

Andrew Robinson found that Clint Adams was right. The steak at the Marble Hall was excellent. He didn't even mind listening to James Wonderly's offer while he was eating it. The fact that the offer was a long, drawn-out one gave Robinson time to finish dinner before he turned Wonderly down.

"What?"

"I said, no thank you, Mr. Wonderly," Robinson said. "I'm going quite nicely on my own."

"Maybe you didn't understand my offer," Wonderly said.

"Oh, you explained it very well. I understand it all perfectly."

"And you're turning me down?"

"Flat."

"I don't understand," Wonderly said. "It's a perfectly good offer. Why would you turn it down?"

"For the simple reasons that I do not want to sell."

"But . . . your store is dying here."

"Then why do *you* want it?"

Wonderly cleared his throat.

"I'm from here," he said hurriedly, "I know the people around here. They'll buy from me."

"Well, they'll buy from me, too," Robinson said. "In fact, we had a customer yesterday and a customer today."

"And what about Adams?"

"What about him?"

"Will he continue to work for you?"

"Until I find someone full-time Mr. Adams has agreed to work in the store for me."

"And what are you paying him?"

"Nothing."

Wonderly wasn't sure he'd heard right.

"Nothing?"

"That's right."

Adams had turned down a job with him, and he was working for this Easterner for nothing? Wonderly's blood began to boil.

"He's a partner, then?"

"No."

"Then why would he work for nothing?"

"You'll have to ask him."

"It makes no sense."

"Again," Robinson said, "you'll have to ask him. Well, thank you for the meal, Mr. Wonderly, and for the interest. I'm sorry we couldn't do business. I think I'll forgo dessert and call it a night." He rose to leave.

Wonderly said, "Maybe you don't understand who I am, Robinson. If you don't do business with me, you don't do business in Kansas City."

"I understand everything all too well, Mr. Wonderly," Robinson said. Then he smiled. "But I doubt that you are that big a man."

"You have no idea how big I am. You come here from back East and think we're all some kind of bumpkins."

"I'm not questioning your business acumen, Mr. Wonderly," Robinson said. "In fact, I'm sure you're a shrewd businessman, and that's why you made your offer. You realize that my store is going to make money. I can't blame you for wanting a piece of the pie—but I do draw the line at giving you the whole pie.''

''But—''

''You know, if you'd made me an offer for a piece I might have considered it.''

''I don't take pieces, Robinson,'' Wonderly said. ''I'm gonna swallow you whole.''

''Good night, Mr. Wonderly.''

Wonderly stood up and shouted at Robinson as he left, ''You're gonna find out just how big I really am!''

Robinson left the Marble Hall without ever turning around.

THIRTY-FOUR

When Clint came out of the café and crossed back to the store he saw that the man had moved down several doorways and taken up a position in front of a hardware store. He unlocked the door, stepped in, locked it, and went upstairs to the rooms of the late Harrison Banbury.

Thanks to Banbury's interest in books Clint had something to while away the time. He chose a volume by Mark Twain and settled down to read it. By the time he looked up it had grown dark enough for him to light the lamp next to his chair. At that moment there was a knock on the door downstairs. He went down, let Andrew Robinson in, and led him back upstairs.

"Do you mind?" Robinson asked, indicating the decanters of wine and brandy.

"Help yourself. I expect you paid for the stuff."

"Join me?"

"No, thanks," Clint said. "Too rich for me. How did dinner go?"

"You were right about the steak," Robinson said. "We were both right about Wonderly."

"He made his offer?"

"A long, long offer," Robinson said. "I didn't even have to put him off until after dinner. He talked the whole time. You know, he's a big man here in Kansas City, but back East they'd chew him up and spit him out.''

''Not so easily, if he did business there the same way he does it here.''

''With violence?''

Clint nodded.

''We can handle violence in Philadelphia and New York, Clint,'' Robinson said grimly.

''What was his reaction when you turned him down?''

Robinson sat down directly across from Clint before answering, holding his brandy snifter delicately in one hand.

''He was angry, to say the least,'' he said. ''He started shouting so everyone could hear him. He said if I didn't do business with him here I wouldn't do business, at all.''

''And what did you tell him?''

''I told him I didn't think he was *that* big.''

''And he was angry before that,'' Clint said. ''After it he must have been enraged.''

''I left.''

''Well, let's hope he considers his next move very carefully. If he gets violent, with a little luck it will be after you leave.''

Robinson swirled the brandy, sniffed it appreciatively, and then drank. ''Harrison had excellent taste.''

''How long did you know him?'' Clint asked.

''Many years,'' Robinson said. ''He worked for my father years ago. When I started my own business I found him and hired him. He had fallen on hard times.''

''He must have appreciated the help,'' Clint said.

''Yes,'' Robinson said, ''I helped him right into an early grave.''

''What happened wasn't your fault.''

''I keep telling myself that.''

He finished his brandy and returned the glass to the small bar.

''I think I'll make it an early night. I have an early train.''

"I'll meet you in the lobby of your hotel."

"All right," Robinson said.

Clint went down with him, shaking Robinson's hand before letting him out. He watched carefully as the Fancy Man's owner walked away to see if anyone followed him. No one did, so he went back upstairs, back to his Mark Twain.

THIRTY-FIVE

When James Wonderly got home he was still incensed. He tore off his tie and made himself a drink. How dare that Eastern bastard turn him down! Robinson was going to learn the hard way what folly that had been. He'd made a generous offer—a *more* than generous offer—that any man in his right mind would have accepted.

He unbuttoned his shirt, sat down, stood up, finished his drink, and poured another one. Even the good Scotch could not ease his anger. When he was wound up like this only one thing could help him. He was sorry he hadn't stopped off and picked up a young whore on his way home. Sex was the way he worked out his anger.

He thought about his wife and how different she had looked earlier in the evening. Attractive, even. It had been some time since they'd shared the same bed, but she was—after all—still his wife.

He poured himself a third drink and carried it upstairs to her door.

He knocked and called her name.

"Stella!"

Stella Wonderly was lying in her bed with her new undergarment on. She was thinking about Clint Adams, had her eyes closed tightly and her hand down between her legs when she heard the knock on her door and her name called. She jerked her hand out from between her thighs as if she'd been burned. She could tell three things from the sound of her husband's voice. One: He was angry. Two: He was drunk. And three: He wanted sex. Why hadn't he brought one of his women home with him? Why was he bothering her?

There was, of course, a time when Stella wanted to have sex with her husband, but that time was long past. Also, she didn't want him to see what she was wearing, because he'd know where it came from and he'd be angry.

"Stella!" He knocked harder. "I want to come in."

"I'm sleepy, James."

Now he pounded on the door with his fist.

"Stella! You're still my wife! You have a duty to perform."

"Not tonight, James."

"Damn it, woman. Open the door before I break it down."

"I have a gun, James," she said. "And I'll use it. I don't want to be bothered with you tonight. Find one of your whores."

"By God, woman—"

"I have a gun, James," she said. "You know I do." She did. It was in the bottom drawer of her dresser. He had bought it for her himself. Little did he—or she—know that she would be threatening him with it years later.

"You bitch!" he said. "You'd shoot me?"

"If you break into my room drunk, yes."

"Bitch," he said, smacking her door once with his open palm. He started down the hall and she heard him mutter, "Bitch," once more.

When she was sure he was gone she closed her eyes, went back to her fantasy about Clint Adams, and slid her hand down between her legs. Even when she and her husband were having sex it had never been like that afternoon with Clint. She and James had *never* had that kind of passion between them. In fact, she didn't think James was capable of that kind of passion at any time in his life.

And certainly not now.

James Wonderly went to his own bedroom and slammed the door. It was too late and he was too tired to go out and find a whore for the night. He'd finish his drink and go to bed, and in the morning he'd figure out what to do about Andrew Robinson, Clint Adams, and the Fancy Man stores.

THIRTY-SIX

Clint rose very early in the morning and went to the Kansas House hotel to wait for Andrew Robinson. He was there no more than ten minutes when the man came walking down the stairs.

"Good morning," he greeted Clint.

"Do you have time for breakfast?" Clint asked.

Robinson checked his watch and said, "I believe I do. Right here?"

"The food is good here."

"All right, then," Robinson said. "The least I can do is buy you breakfast."

"I won't argue with that."

"And we can talk about your wages."

After they were seated and had ordered their breakfasts Clint said, "Who said anything about wages?"

"Well, actually, it was Wonderly," Robinson said. "He asked me what I was paying you, and I had to say nothing—which isn't fair."

"I haven't asked to be paid," Clint pointed out.

"But if I had someone else running the store I'd be paying them."

"Did Banbury have any family?"

"No, none."

Clint had thought to have Robinson pay him, but send the money to the dead man's family.

"You have to eat and earn a living while you're helping me, Clint," Robinson said. "At least let me pay you what I was paying Harrison."

"Fine," Clint said. "Have it deposited in the Bank of Denver. I have an account there."

"All right," Robinson said. "I feel better now."

Clint would decide later what he'd do with the money. He would probably donate it to a worthy cause.

After breakfast Clint walked Robinson over to the railroad station. He checked the street but no one was watching them. He had a feeling there was a man waiting for him at the store, though. No one had been there when he left, but someone would be by opening time.

"Make sure you tell Roper what's going on when you get to Denver," Clint said. "He'll make sure you're safe while you're there."

"You really think Wonderly can reach out that far for me?"

"He has money," Clint said. "He thinks he can reach anywhere with it. Some wealthy men are like that—present company excepted, I assume."

The train whistle blew so Clint and Robinson stepped up onto the platform.

"I'm not so sure I am an exception," the man said. "I suppose I have done some things I'm not proud of."

"We all have," Clint agreed.

The two men shook hands and then stood back as the train pulled in. Robinson—traveling light with one bag—stepped up on to the train. He waved once and went inside.

After the train pulled out Clint went straight back to the store. He didn't like leaving it unattended for any period of time. On his way back, walking on Broadway, he saw Eileen Wilson coming toward him. She was obviously on her way to work at Wonderly's office.

"Good morning, Miss Wilson," he said, tipping his hat.

"Mr. Adams."

"I trust your boss's business dinner with Mr. Robinson went well?"

"I have not seen Mr. Wonderly yet so I don't know how it went," she said. "I suppose I'll find out when he gets to the office."

"Do you usually arrive at his office first?"

"Yes," she said, "Mr. Wonderly insists that I be there promptly by nine."

"And when does he come in?"

"Whenever he pleases," she said. "It's his office. Now, if you'll excuse me."

"Miss Wilson," he said, "you disappoint me."

"I beg your pardon?"

"You still harbor a grudge against me."

"I hold no grudge," she denied in a frosty tone.

"But you treat me as if you do."

"I hardly know you, Mr. Adams—"

"And I'd like to remedy that, Miss Wilson, by taking you to dinner."

"I think not."

"Why not?"

"I just—"

"—hold a grudge," he finished for her.

"I don't!" she said. "I'm not a . . . a spiteful person."

"If that were true," Clint said, "you would consent to have dinner with me."

"Mr. Adams—"

"Prove me wrong, then," he said.

She studied him for a few moments, and then said, "Oh, very well."

"I will call for you at your home this evening. Where do you live?" he asked belatedly.

"I don't know you well enough to tell you that, Mr. Adams."

"All right, then," he said. "Meet me at the Marble Hall at seven."

"Seven-thirty would be more suitable."

"Very well, then," he said. "Seven-thirty. It's a date."

"Now I must go to work."

"I wouldn't want you to be late, Miss Wilson," he said, "or can I call you Eileen?"

"Miss Wilson will do for now," she said, and walked on.

Maybe she wouldn't give him her address or let him call her by her first name yet, but he hoped that would all be different after dinner tonight.

He realized, of course, that he was guilty of the same thing Wonderly was when he was invited to the Marble Hall. Trying to use the place to impress her.

He'd have to talk to Joe Bassett and make sure he was treated the same way tonight as he had been when he met Wonderly there.

THIRTY-SEVEN

James Wonderly arrived at his office in a foul mood. Not even the sight of Miss Wilson bending over to file a piece of paper was enough to bring him out of it.

"Miss Wilson!"

"Yes, sir?"

"I want everything you can find on Andrew Robinson and the Fancy Man stores, even if you have to spend all day at the telegraph office."

"Yes, sir."

"And if you have to work late do that, too."

"Oh . . ."

"What is it?"

"Well . . . I did have a dinner engagement."

"With a beau, Miss Wilson?" he asked.

"Hardly, sir."

"Well, business is much more important, don't you think?"

"Yes, sir . . ."

"Who was this dinner with?" Now Wonderly was curious as to who Miss Wilson deemed proper dinner company.

"Uh, well, it's with Clint Adams, sir."

"Clint Adams? You're having dinner with Clint Adams?" he demanded.

"Yes, sir," she said. "I didn't see the harm. He's been trying to make it up to me ever since—"

"No, no," Wonderly said, suddenly struck by an idea. "No, I think it's fine. You have your dinner with Mr. Adams. What time is it supposed to take place?"

"Seven-thirty," she said. "I'm to meet him at the Marble Hall at seven-thirty."

"Well, you get as much work done for me as you can by six, and then you go home and get yourself all pretty for your dinner."

"Yes, sir . . . although it's really not that kind of dinner—"

"And see if you can locate Les Revere for me."

She made a face and said, "Yes, sir," as Wonderly went into his office.

Locating Les Revere was not one of Eileen Wilson's favorite pastimes.

James Wonderly felt better as he closed the door of his office. He knew where Clint Adams was gong to be at seven-thirty that evening. That was a piece of information that was going to come in very handy indeed.

THIRTY-EIGHT

There were two customers that day, both women about Stella's age. Clint assumed that she had sent them. He also assumed she had not told them what had happened in the storeroom, because neither woman asked to try any garments on. In any case, neither of these women were as attractive as Doreen or Stella. They both spoke of surprising their husbands, and Clint was sure that the husbands would appreciate the effort their wives were making.

Four customers in three days. Things were looking up for the Fancy Man.

And James Wonderly wouldn't like that one bit.

"... two more customers today," Revere said to Wonderly.

"That doesn't matter," he said.

"And Robinson left this morning on an early train to Denver."

"That doesn't matter, either."

"What's going on?"

"Our Miss Wilson is having dinner with Clint Adams tonight."

"And that's good?"

"It's good," Wonderly said, "because we know where he'll be at seven-thirty."

"And?"

"And you can pay a visit to the store," Wonderly said. "You and your men."

"These men hired on to fight, Mr. Wonderly," Revere said, "not to vandalize a store."

"I'm paying them enough to do whatever I want them to do, Revere!" Wonderly snapped. "Besides, what do you think they'll have to do once Adams sees what happened to the store?"

Revere thought about that for a moment and then said, "He'll probably come after us."

"And you'll be justified in shooting him down."

"This might work," Revere said.

"Of course it will work," James Wonderly said. "It's perfect."

As Revere left the office he gave Eileen Wilson a leer that made her skin crawl.

"Enjoy your dinner tonight," he said.

She frowned. The only way he could have known about her dinner with Clint Adams was if her boss had told him.

Why would Mr. Wonderly do that?

Clint closed the store a few minutes early. Having dinner with Eileen Wilson was a calculated risk to the store, but on top of the fact that she was incredibly lovely and he wanted to see her in one of the Fancy Man items, she was close to James Wonderly. She might have some idea of what he was planning, and although she'd probably never give anything away, it was possible she might let something slip.

He was just going to have to hope that he didn't end up trying to explain to Andrew Robinson why he had taken a few hours away from the store to have dinner with a lovely woman.

He went upstairs to dress for their dinner and suddenly had the urge for a glass of Harrison C. Banbury's expensive port.

It would get the night off on the right foot.

THIRTY-NINE

Clint got to the Marble Hall first and was greeted by Kern.

"What, again?"

"I didn't get to eat last time."

"Another big meeting?"

"Dinner with a lady."

"Ah," Kern said, with a twinkle in his eyes. "And would you like the same kind of treatment we gave you last time?"

"It wouldn't hurt," Clint said.

Kern patted his arm and said, "I'll have your regular waiter come over and take your regular order."

"That's fine."

"And Mr. Bassett himself will come to your table and meet the young lady."

"Joe's probably busy," Clint said.

"Never too busy to visit the table of one of our favorite patrons," Kern said. "Leave it to me. Should I show you to your table?"

"Sure, why not?"

"Luckily, your regular table is open."

Clint followed Kern to the same table he had sat at with James Wonderly.

"When the lady arrives," Kern said, "I'll show her to your table personally."

"You're too kind."

"Would you like anything in the meanwhile?"

"No," Clint said, "I'll wait for the lady."

"A true gentleman."

"By the way, her name is Eileen Wilson."

"I'll be on the lookout for Miss Wilson."

Kern withdrew and Clint had a look around the room. The place was only half filled and when the next diner appeared in the doorway Clint recognized him immediately.

James Wonderly.

The man never looked over at Clint's table while he was being shown to his own. Clint wondered if Eileen Wilson had told her boss about their dinner. But why would she? Was he being set up.

Ten minutes later Kern appeared at the doorway, leading Eileen. It was the first time Clint had seen her in anything but one of her business outfits, and she looked stunning. She was a wearing a dress that, while not especially revealing, was tight enough to show off what she had. All the male eyes in the place followed her to his table—except those of her boss. Clint decided that Wonderly was studiously avoiding looking over at them.

Clint stood up as Kern and Eileen reached the table.

"Mr. Adams," Kern said formally, "your charming dinner companion has arrived."

"I can see that," Clint said, and so could all the other men in the place. "You look absolutely lovely."

"Thank you."

"Allow me," Kern said, and held her chair for her.

"Thank you," she repeated as she seated herself.

"Mr. Adams, I'll have your regular waiter come right over."

"Thank you, Kern."

As Kern left Eileen said, "I didn't know you were so well known here—and well thought of. That man absolutely lit up when I told him who I was here to dine with.''

''I don't get here very often,'' Clint admitted, ''but when I do they treat me very well. What would you like to drink when the waiter comes?''

''A glass of wine would be nice.''

''Any particular kind?''

''Oh, no,'' she said. ''I'm not particular. I like wines, but I don't know them. Anything red will be fine.''

''I notice your boss is eating here tonight.''

''Is he?'' She looked around and then spotted Wonderly. ''I see that he is. Well, he dines here quite often.''

Clint didn't say anything.

''All right,'' she said, suddenly, ''I told him I would be meeting you here.''

''Did you?''

''Yes,'' she said, ''but only because he wanted me to work late.''

''I see.''

''But he relented and allowed me to go home to change for dinner.''

''How nice of him.''

''You two don't get along, do you?''

''No, we don't.''

''Why is that?''

''How much do you know about your boss's business, Eileen?'' Clint asked instead.

''As much as he tells me,'' she said. ''I file papers for him, do research, but I really don't know much about what he does.''

''Or how?''

''His methods are his own business.''

''What's the last thing he asked you to research—if I may ask?''

''I don't see why not,'' she said. ''It was your friend Mr. Robinson and his Fancy Man stores.''

''Really?''

"That was just today," she said. "He was quite surprised."

"Why's that?"

"Well, I don't think he knew just what a wealthy family Mr. Robinson comes from. I know he's been fairly upset about Mr. Robinson turning down an offer he made to buy him out. I suppose now he knows why."

"Tell me," Clint said, "how did he react to the news that Robinson is richer than he is?"

"Not well," she replied, "not well at all."

"Good," Clint said, and the waiter appeared and cut off their conversation.

FORTY

They did not speak of Wonderly again until they were into their meal. Clint noticed that Wonderly had been served at almost the same time. The man continued to sit with his back to them, and never turned around to look at them.

"What do you think of the men your boss employs?"

"I detest one in particular."

"Oh? Who's that?"

"Les Revere."

"Why?"

"He . . . looks at me in a way I find . . . reprehensible."

"I agree he's not the nicest man you'd ever want to meet."

She laughed.

"You have a gift for understatement. He's awful! And those other men he brought to town."

"Others?"

"Three more, just like him. They came to the office once and all three looked at me in the same . . . filthy way. They're just like him."

"So they came to see Wonderly?"

"Just once," she said. "Now they only deal with Revere."

"Do you know why they're here?"

"Well . . . I think it has something to do with you."

"How is your food?" Clint abruptly changed the subject.

"This is the best veal I've ever had," she said. "I must admit I've never eaten here before."

"Your boss has never brought you here?"

She shook her head.

"Well, I'll see that you're treated well if you ever want to come back."

"Oh," she said, "I could never afford to eat here on my salary."

"Wonderly doesn't pay you well?"

"Oh, don't misunderstand," she said. "He pays me well—just not well enough to eat here regularly."

"Well, you can eat here any time you want, and I'll have them put it on my bill."

"Oh, that's very nice of you, but I couldn't—"

"I'm sure they'd enjoy having you here," he said. "You brighten the place up."

She looked down shyly and said, "Thank you."

They finished their dinner and Clint asked if she would like dessert. They both ordered pie and coffee. Along with the dessert came a visit from Joe Bassett, who was extremely charming to Eileen and respectful to Clint. When he shook Clint's hand prior to leaving he turned his back to Eileen and winked.

Across the room Wonderly was still lingering over his dinner.

"Does it bother you to have him here?" she asked.

"What?"

"You keep looking over at Mr. Wonderly," she said. "It's not very flattering."

"I'm sorry," he said. "I'm just wondering why he's here."

"To eat dinner?"

"He was served before us, and is still eating," Clint pointed out. "He's stalling."

"Stalling? Why would he do that?"

"Did he talk to Revere today?"

"As a matter of fact, he did. Right after I told him about my dinner with you he told me to find Revere."

"Tell me again how he reacted to hearing that you were dining with me."

"Well, he seemed surprised and was telling me I had to work late . . . and then, abruptly, he changed his tune."

"He did?"

"Seemingly for no reason, he insisted that I leave early enough to keep my . . . my engagement with you. He was very insistent."

Suddenly, Clint was sure he had made a mistake—and maybe a fatal one for the Fancy Man.

"Eileen, would you mind if we left now?"

"You haven't finished your pie."

"I have a bad feeling . . ."

"About what?"

"I think I've made a mistake."

"By being here with me?"

"No . . . no, it would take too long to explain now, but—"

He was cut off by someone rushing into the dining room.

"Fire!" the man yelled. "We got a real bad fire goin' on!"

"Where?" someone shouted.

But Clint knew the answer even before the man said, "Thirteenth Street. We think it's that new Fancy store."

FORTY-ONE

Clint and Eileen stood together across the street while the fire department was fighting the blaze. They were simply trying to douse the fire now, before it could spread. There was no hope of saving the Fancy Man.

"This is my fault," Clint said.

"How?" Eileen asked. "Why?"

"I wanted to have dinner with you, impress you," he said. "If I'd been here this wouldn't have happened."

"Well," she said, "when you put it that way, it could be my fault."

"No," Clint said, "actually, it's your boss's fault."

"How do you figure that? He was at the restaurant where we were. We saw him."

"That was the point," Clint said. "That's why he ate there, because you told him we'd be there. That's why he was stalling over his meal. To give Revere time to set this fire."

"But . . . Mr. Wonderly made an offer to buy this store. Why would he want it burned down?"

"Because he offered to buy it and was turned down," Clint said.

"But that's ridiculous!" she exclaimed. "He makes offers, makes business deals all the time. Some are successful, some aren't. He can't burn out everyone who refuses him."

"Can't he?"

She touched his arm.

"Clint, I'm sorry about the store burning down. I'm sorry it happened while we were dining together, but I think it's a little suspicious of you to blame it on Mr. Wonderly . . . don't you?"

"No," Clint stated, "I don't. Come on, Eileen, I'll walk you home. If we stay here too long the smell of the smoke will get into your clothes and your hair."

"That's all right," she said. "You can stay—"

"Why?" he asked, cutting her off. "There's nothing left to see, and all my clothes have gone up in smoke."

"Where will you stay?"

"I'll go back to the hotel where I was before."

"Do you have money?"

"The important things are always on me," he said. "I have my money and my gun."

"Your gun is one of the more important things to you?" she asked.

"Oh, yes," he said, "especially when I'm dealing with vermin like Les Revere."

They started to walk away together.

"Now, I can believe that Revere might be capable of setting this fire," she said, "but why would he?"

"Why would he? Because he was told to do it by his boss . . . your boss."

She shook her head as they turned the corner and got away from the smoke.

"I still find it hard to believe that Mr. Wonderly would ever order such a thing."

"I don't think Revere would have thought of it on his own," Clint said. "I don't know that he's capable of that kind of thinking."

"I'd have to agree with you there."

They walked several blocks and then she had them turn

right. After several more blocks they were in a residential section.

"It's right here," she said, stopping in front of a house. "I have a room upstairs."

He could see that her eyes were still tearing from the smoke.

"I'm sorry about your eyes and the smoke," he said.

"I'll be fine," she said. "How about you?"

"I'll have some explaining to do to Mr. Robinson about how I let his store burn down," he said.

"But how are you?"

"I'll be fine."

"Are you going to go after Revere?"

"I don't know what I'm going to do," Clint said. "I'll have to think it over."

"Please don't do anything rash."

"Me? Rash? Have you ever known me to be rash?"

"Well, you did charge into Mr. Wonderly's office that day."

"Ah," he said, "but that was a well-thought-out action."

"It was?"

"Oh, yes."

"Well . . . don't make any more well-thought-out moves like that, then."

"I'll think about it."

"Good night."

"Good night."

She started toward the house, then turned and walked back. "You know," she said, "you're really not such a terrible man." She kissed him on the cheek.

"I've known that all along," he said, and she laughed. She started up the walk again and he called out after her, "I just wanted *you* to know it."

FORTY-TWO

The next morning Clint had a talk with Sheriff Atkins.

"You can't prove that fire was set," Atkins said.

"And if I could," Clint retorted, "you still wouldn't do anything about it, would you?"

Atkins surprised Clint and answered the question honestly.

"No, I guess I wouldn't," the man said. "Not if it meant going up against Mr. Wonderly."

"Well, Sheriff," Clint said, "I don't have that problem. I'm going to prove that he had that fire set, and that he had Harrison Banbury killed."

"Who?"

"The man who used to run the Fancy Man store."

"Oh, him."

"Yes, him. I think he deserves to be remembered, don't you?"

"Adams," Atkins said, "what do you want me to do?"

"I want you to stay out of my way, Sheriff," Clint warned. "I don't want to go up against you because you're the law, so stay out of my way."

"What are you gonna do?"

"I told you already. I'm going after Revere and his men, and James Wonderly."

"I have to live here, Adams—"

"I'm not asking you for any help, Sheriff," Clint said, and then added, "Just stay out of my way."

As Clint went out the door Atkins muttered, "Don't you worry, I will."

James Wonderly felt a wonderful sense of satisfaction. The Fancy Man was gone. *That should teach both Clint Adams and Andrew Robinson a lesson,* he thought gleefully.

"Here's that file you asked for, Mr. Wonderly."

He was in such an expansive mood that he decided to make his move with Miss Wilson.

"Miss Wilson, how long have you worked here?"

"About six months."

"Do you like your job?"

"Very much."

"Do you like me?"

Eileen hesitated, then said, "Sir?"

"I asked if you liked me."

"Well, sir . . . you're my boss."

"That doesn't mean you have to like me," Wonderly said. "Tell me, do you find me attractive?"

"Mr. Wonderly," Eileen said, "I don't think this is an appropriate conversation . . . I mean, you're married, and I work for you—"

He came around his desk and moved close to her—too close for her comfort. In fact, he reached for her, put his hands on her waist.

"Eileen," he said, "I find you very attractive, and I have a lot of money. I could make you . . . very comfortable."

"Mr. Wonderly—"

"Call me James," he said, and put one hand on her right breast.

She slapped him, even before she knew what she was going to do.

"Stop that!" she snapped.

"You bitch!" he said, eyes blazing, grabbing her arm. "You know you want it—"

She stomped on his foot and he released her. She backed away from him, throwing the file down on the floor.

"I quit!" she shouted. "You're a horrible man."

"Get out then, you ungrateful bitch," he snapped. "There are plenty of women out there who could do your job. Get out!"

"I'm going!"

She turned and stormed out of the office, stopping short when she saw Clint.

"You were right about him," she said. "He's a horrible man."

"Are you all right?"

"I'm fine," she said. "I'm going home. Will you come and see me later?"

"Of course."

"Thank you," she said, and left.

As Clint entered Wonderly's office the man was bent over, massaging his foot.

"That bitch—"

"That's not a nice way to talk about a lady, Wonderly." Clint said.

Wonderly looked up swiftly at the sound of his voice—obviously he was expecting someone else, probably Revere, Clint suspected.

"Get out of my office, Adams—" he started, but Clint swept the man's left foot out from under him; since he was standing only on that foot, massaging the right, he fell onto his ass.

"What the—"

Clint picked him up by his shirtfront and backhanded him across the face. The blow knocked Wonderly ass over teakettle across his desk and onto the floor on the other side of it.

"Are you mad?" Wonderly sputtered.

Clint didn't answer. He walked around the desk and

lifted the man to his feet again. Physically, the man was no match for him.

Clint grabbed him by the lapels of his jacket and rammed him into the large window behind him. The glass shattered and he pushed Wonderly through it, maintaining the hold on his jacket.

"What the—are you crazy?" Wonderly screamed, as he dangled out the window.

"The fall won't kill you, Wonderly," Clint said, pulling the man back in, "unless you land on your head. My guess is you'll break an arm or a leg."

"You wouldn't dare—I'll have you arrested."

"Atkins has been warned to stay out of my way, and that's what he'll do. You killed Banbury, Wonderly, and you burned the store to the ground. Maybe the law isn't going to touch you, but I won't let you get away with it."

Wonderly sneered and said, "What can you do?"

"This," Clint replied, and pushed the man out the window and let him go.

Clint went downstairs and found Wonderly lying on the ground, surrounded by a crowd asking what happened. Clint walked to the fallen man and loomed over him.

"Jesus . . ." Wonderly moaned, grimacing in pain. Clint didn't know if it was the man's arm, leg, or back that was hurting, and he didn't care.

"You're a dead man," Wonderly said to him, gasping, "a dead man . . . Jesus, somebody get me a doctor!"

FORTY-THREE

Chappy was beside himself with laughter.

"You threw him out his window?"

"That's right."

"Jesus, I wish I'd been there to see that," the bartender said. "Is he dead?"

"No," Clint said. "Last I saw he was being carried to the doctor. I think he broke his leg."

"*You* broke his leg!" Chappy said, and started laughing again. "You threw him through . . . a window!"

"Yes, I did."

"That's worth a free beer."

When Clint had his beer Chappy said, "I guess the sheriff'll be coming for you."

"No, he won't," Clint replied. "He's already been warned to stay out of my way."

"Well then, Revere will be coming for you, that's for sure."

Clint grinned tightly and said, "That's what I'm counting on."

"Oh, I get it," Chappy said. "When they come for you, you'll be ready. But what about Wonderly? You gonna be happy with just pushing him through a window?"

"I don't know, Chappy," Clint said. "I guess we'll just have to wait and see."

Wonderly sat in his living room with his broken leg propped up on a chair.

"You heard me, Revere," he said. "I want him dead. Take your men and kill him."

"But he threw you out a window," Revere said. "When he's dead don't you think people will think—"

"I don't care what people think," Wonderly said, cutting Revere off. "I just want Clint Adams dead by nightfall. Understand? *Dead.*"

"I understand, Mr. Wonderly," Revere said. "I understand."

After Les Revere left, Stella Wonderly came down the stairs from the second floor, where she had been listening to the conversation. She headed for the front door, as well.

"Stella."

She kept walking.

"Stella! Get me some coffee."

She opened the front door.

"Stella, damn it—"

"Get your own coffee, James!" she finally shouted at him. "I'm finished with you. You can't just order people killed, you know. Who do you think you are that you can burn people out or order them killed?"

"Where do you think you're going?" he demanded.

"Away," she said. "Away from you."

"If you leave you can't come back, do you hear? I won't take you back!"

"I don't care," Stella Wonderly said. "I'm not coming back."

With that she went out the door.

Clint waited on the front porch for Eileen Wilson to come out. When she did she looked miserable.

"I can't believe it," she said, shaking her head. "What happened to make him do something like that?"

"He'd just been waiting for the chance, Eileen," Clint said. "Don't you see? That's why he hired you."

"I suppose . . ."

"Will you be all right?"

"Oh, yes," she said. "I'll be able to get another job. I'm just angry that I could be fooled like that."

"Don't be," Clint said. "Men like that fool a lot of people."

"What about your business with him?" she asked. She still had no idea that after she left he had thrown Wonderly through his window. "Is it finished?"

"Not quite," he said. "I think there's just one more thing to be done."

FORTY-FOUR

Clint went to the Kansas House so that Revere and his men wouldn't have any trouble finding him. He didn't know all of Revere's men. He had seen them from across the street, and had come face-to-face with that one man in the doorway of the café, but he had no idea who they were or how well they could handle a gun. He just felt sure that anyone who would work for Wonderly and Revere couldn't be anyone with any spine. Burning a building down at night was a cowardly way to go about things, and who knew if the men were even aware he hadn't been inside? If they weren't, and they thought they were burning him, too, it made it even more of an act of cowardice.

Clint never worried about facing cowards, no matter their numbers. He'd faced four-to-one odds before, against better opposition, and lived to tell the tale.

He was surprised when he saw the woman, Stella, enter the lobby of the hotel. She appeared disheveled, as if she'd been running.

"Stella? Wha—"

"Wonderly."

"What?"

"That's my last name," She said. "I'm Stella Wonderly."

"You're . . . James Wonderly's wife?" Clint was flabbergasted.

"That's right."

"But why—"

"I wanted to hurt him," she said. "I wanted to meet the man who was causing him so much distress. There are a lot of reasons I came to the store that day, but none of them have anything to do with today. I've come to warn you, Clint. James has sent Revere and his men to kill you."

"I know."

"You—know?"

"Well, I figured he would, after I pushed him through that window."

"It's true, then?" she asked. "You really threw him out a window?"

"Well, through it, actually," Clint said.

She started to laugh, almost uncontrollably.

"Stella!" He grabbed her by the shoulders and shook her.

"Oh, it's all right, Clint," she said. "I'm not hysterical. I'm fine. In fact, I'm more than fine. I just walked out on my husband."

"Like this?" he asked. "With nothing?"

"I don't want anything," she said. "I just wanted to get away, and I have—finally, after all these years, I have."

He was going to say something else but at that moment Les Revere appeared at the front door of the hotel.

"Stella," Clint said, pressing his room key into her hand, "go upstairs and wait for me."

"Why?" she asked, then turned and saw Revere. "Oh, my God—"

"Go ahead," he said, "go on up, and don't come down until I call you."

"But—"

"Go!"

She made a face but left him standing there.

Clint waited until Stella was safely upstairs before walking over to where Revere was standing.

"You still smell of smoke, Les," he said.

Revere frowned and sniffed himself before he realized he was giving himself away.

"Very smart, Adams," Revere said. "So what are you gonna do about it?"

"Do you have your men with you?"

"They're outside."

"In the middle of the street?" Clint asked. "Or hiding?"

"They don't have to hide."

"Will it be three against one," Clint asked, "or four?"

Revere smiled.

"I wouldn't miss this for the world."

"Well, go on out and I'll be there in a minute," Clint said. "Oh, and make sure you're all in the street. I don't want to have to come looking for you."

Revere frowned.

"You're just gonna come out and face us?"

"Why not?"

"There are four of us."

"I thought I already said that."

"Wait a minute. You want us all in the street so you can sneak out the back door," Revere accused.

Clint shook his head and said, "Not my style at all, Les. No, I'll be out in the street."

"To face all four of us."

"Right."

"At one time?"

"Yes."

"And you're not worried?"

"Should I be?"

"I would be."

"Fortunately," Clint said, "I'm not you."

"I don't get it," Revere said, looking puzzled.

"You will," Clint said, "believe me, you will."

• • •

Les Revere went back out into the street where his three men were waiting.

"Well?" one of them demanded. "Is he there?"

"He's there."

"Is he coming out?" the second one asked.

"He says he is."

"Maybe he's going out the back door," the third man said.

"No," Revere said, "he's gonna come out and face all four of us, and he ain't worried about it."

The other three men exchanged glances.

"He can't be as good as they say he is," the first man said.

"Can he?" the second man asked.

Now all four of them exchanged glances, and then turned to look at the hotel. They waited quietly, each entertained by their own thoughts.

Clint waited inside the hotel, giving the four men time to think about what was going to happen. When he figured they'd had long enough for their imaginations to run wild he stepped out the door.

FORTY-FIVE

The four men were standing abreast in the street, little more than an arm's length between them, Les Revere second from Clint's right. Clint stopped just in the doorway to take a good look, and to give them more time to think things over. Two of them were flexing their gun hands, one of them was fidgeting from foot to foot. The only one standing stock-still was Revere, and Clint thought this was because he was too stupid to be nervous. That meant he'd have to go first.

Clint left the doorway, stepping down into the street. Foot traffic suddenly stopped, and people began to congregate on both sides of the street. Someone stepped out into the street on both ends and began stopping horses and buggies and wagons. The street was clear for what was to happen next.

"You boys have one chance to change your minds and ride out," Clint called out. "I can't be any fairer than that."

"We're not goin' anywhere, Adams," Revere said. "Are we, boys?"

The other three didn't answer.

"Remember how much you're bein' paid!" Revere said.

The air was staticky with tension, and then one of them said, "I ain't gettin' paid enough to die."

He had been fidgeting from foot to foot, and now he backed away from the action with his hands held away from his guns.

"Three to one," Clint said to Revere. "Your odds are shrinking, Revere."

"His money goes to you two," Revere said. "Get him!"

The two men froze. It wasn't normal for one man to willingly face four, not unless he was crazy—or simply that good.

"Draw on him, I said!"

"They're waiting for you to make the first move, Revere," Clint goaded him. "Come on, show them what you're made of."

"All right," Revere said, "then draw when I do . . . now!"

Clint knew Revere would draw. He was too dumb not to. Clint cleared leather first. Revere was slow enough that he had time to put a bullet in the man's right kneecap.

The other two men hesitated so long that they were hopelessly beat. Clint fired at their feet, and they both threw their hands up in the air.

"Guns on the ground," Clint said.

Both men plucked their weapons from their holsters and dropped them to the ground.

"You, too!" Clint shouted to the third man, who did the same.

Clint walked toward Revere, who was sitting on the ground, holding both hands over his shattered knee. Ribbons of blood seeped between his fingers.

"Jesus—" he said, his face shiny with sweat.

Clint turned toward the other men.

"We did what you said, Mr. Adams," one of them said. "We dropped 'em."

"Were you boys at the fire last night?"

"Yes, sir."

"You're going to have to talk to a Federal marshal."

They were silent.

"You'll talk to a marshal or pick up your guns and we'll finish this."

"N-no," one of them said. "We'll talk to him."

Clint looked down at Revere.

"Les? You want to take the blame for all of this alone? Killing Banbury, setting the fire. Trying to kill me?"

"He'll get me off," Revere said. "He'll buy me off."

"To do that," Clint said, "he'd have to care about you. You tell me . . . does he?"

Clint waited a few minutes for Revere's answer, then used his boot to prod the man's injured leg.

Revere hissed in pain and said, "Yeah, yeah, I'll talk."

Clint had not yet sent a telegram about the fire to Andrew Robinson. Now at least he had some good news to give him, too.

James Wonderly was going to pay for everything he had done—and not at all in the way he usually did.

Watch for

THE LAST BOUNTY

208th novel in the exciting GUNSMITH series
from Jove

Coming in May!